WILD KNIGHT

MIDNIGHT EMPIRE: THE TOWER, BOOK 1

ANNABEL CHASE

RED PALM PRESS LLC

Copyright © 2021 by Annabel Chase

All rights reserved.

No part of this book may be reproduced in any form or by any electronic or mechanical means, including information storage and retrieval systems, without written permission from the author, except for the use of brief quotations in a book review.

❦ Created with Vellum

1

The only things that ran underground these days were criminals and monsters.

And me, apparently.

I halted outside the entrance to what was once the London Underground station for Edgware Road. The Underground's nickname was 'the Tube,' which seemed fitting, although it was hard to imagine all those trains running below the city. Then again, it was hard to imagine a lot of things about the past. It helped that my mother had been a teacher of history and instilled its importance in me. What we fail to remember, we're condemned to repeat and all that.

"Found him," I said to Minka, my colleague on the other end of the phone.

"He isn't going anywhere. Come back and restock from the armory first."

"And give him time to move? No way." I'd spent hours tracking this guy and I wasn't about to let him go. I wanted to finish this job today.

Minka sighed into the phone. I was personally responsible for the added carbon dioxide in the air thanks to the many, many times I forced a sigh from Minka.

"London, you don't know what's down there."

"Nope."

Only a fool would venture underground without backup and only a grade-A moron would go underground without a weapon.

Did it count that I had a weapon a scant two hours ago but broke it in an unexpected tussle with a pack of pygmy hydras? Technically the mace belonged to the Knights of Boudica and wasn't a favorite of mine. I dispatched the heads with the mace, burned the stumps, and moved on to find my target.

A raven swooped down from the sky, a fresh inkblot spreading across a gray page. The bird perched on top of the entrance and cocked his head.

I lowered the phone. "Don't look at me like that, Barnaby. I'm a big girl and I make my own decisions."

The raven didn't have to respond with "yes, bad ones." I could see the answer in his beady, judgmental eyes.

"Caw, ca-caw."

"Whatever. You stay here. It's too dangerous down there for birds." I raised the phone to my mouth. "I'm going down. See you in an hour."

The voice on the other end of the line shrieked in protest and I held the phone away from my ear.

"What was that? I can't hear you. Too busy getting eaten by whatever monster awaits me. Good-bye, cruel world!"

I secured the phone in its holster on my utility belt and took a quick drink of water from my flask before I sallied forth. If you couldn't sally forth, could you even call yourself a knight?

I entered beneath the sign marked Edgware Road

Station. When the city was still known as London, Edgware Road was a sprawling underground station where city commuters converged to start and end their workday. When humans were still in charge. The arrival of the Eternal Night changed all that.

I slid down the handrail of a defunct escalator and gave my eyes a chance to adjust to the absence of light. Busy city streets had the benefit of electric lights to create the illusion of daytime. Down here was a black ocean and I was already drowning. Good thing I knew how to swim.

My phone vibrated once and fell silent. Minka was probably trying to call me again, to reiterate her warnings and threaten me with bodily harm should I survive. The further I sank, the less likely technology was to work. Another downside of traveling underground.

Still, a job was a job and I needed to eat, preferably today.

A rat the size of a feral hog thundered past me, forcing my back against the wall. The species flourished during the Eternal Night and now they ran rampant above and below ground, carrying disease and scaring the daylights out of us.

Technically daylight was already long gone thanks to the simultaneous eruption of ten of the world's supervolcanoes, an event now referred to as the Great Eruption. The Americas and Australasia were the areas hardest hit because of the locations of the active calderas. Together they spat enough ash into the atmosphere to block the sun. The never-ending eclipse wasn't the only consequence. Magma and monsters spilled forth from the bowels of the earth where they'd been lurking for centuries, biding their time until they could return. And return they did—with a vengeance.

The crackle of my phone cut through the silence. I

reached one hand to the side and pressed the off button. No need to alert anyone to my arrival. The mark himself wasn't particularly dangerous—it was not knowing what else I might encounter along the way that ratcheted up the threat level. There was a reason this job was handed to me and not one of the other knights. To be fair, Kami could've handled it too, but she was nursing a wound from her meeting yesterday with two dwarf factions to negotiate a new boundary between their neighborhoods. Needless to say, it didn't go well. Kami and both parties limped away with injuries. They should've sent Briar instead. Briar radiated warmth whereas Kami radiated do-it-my-way-or-I'll-kill-you-and-feed-you-to-my-cat. Minka was in charge of the schedule, though, and she was reluctant to accept input. The Knights of Boudica were a democracy steeped in bureaucracy and Minka owned the largest roll of red tape.

Out of the corner of my eye, I noticed a flurry of movement. It was small and airborne, and could've been something as insignificant as a moth.

Please don't be a butterfly.

It amazed me that butterflies were once considered pretty and harmless creatures, yet bats were associated with vampires. A glimpse at the right history books revealed that some cultures knew better—to them butterflies represented a departed soul, which was close enough to the truth. In Britannia City, if you saw a swarm of butterflies coming toward you, there was no use running. You were already dead.

Slowly I craned my neck for a better glimpse of my underground companion. A fly landed on the wall of the tunnel and my shoulders relaxed slightly.

I followed the curve of the tunnel and noticed an offshoot. Hmm. Which way next?

A low growl reverberated from the offshoot. The hair on the back of my neck stood at attention.

Offshoot it is.

"Great. More company," I sang out, moving toward the sound. "Come out and join the party. The more the merrier."

Saliva pooled on the tunnel floor with a satisfying hiss. Two red eyes glowed in the darkness.

Make that four.

Shit. Six.

Three large jaws with gleaming fangs quickly followed. A three-headed dog like Cerberus, except this one was protecting a lowlife criminal instead of the god of the underworld. If you ask me, she got the short end of the stick. Then again, she was a dog, so maybe she didn't care which end it was as long as it was a stick.

The dog was about three feet high and as wide as she was tall thanks to the multiple heads. Her black hair was short and coarse and sharp claws extended from her large paws. Not your friendly neighborhood Rover.

I maintained eye contact with the beast. Technically I chose the middle head and focused on that particular pair of eyes.

"Hey, cutie. What's your name?"

"The name's Mongrel and it's about to feast on your flesh for dinner," a gravelly voice said.

"Mongrel? That's a terrible name."

"For a terrible monster," the voice replied.

The three-headed dog punctuated the remark with a round of ferocious barks.

"I take it you're Fergal."

"What's it to you?"

"Come out where I can see you." I didn't dare take

another step forward and irk the dog. The last thing I wanted to do was hurt her. It wasn't her fault she'd been misled into protecting a thief and a liar. Guys like Fergal often withheld food and water as part of the creature's 'training.'

"You're not too bright coming down here alone," Fergal said.

"You're not too bright living down here alone."

I took the opportunity to move closer for a better view of my mark. He was a bulky man in a plain white T-shirt and shredded jeans that hung low on his waist, emphasizing his swollen gut. His thick, knotted hair looked like it hadn't been combed in decades.

"Except I'm not alone. As you can see, I've got Mongrel."

"I'm not alone either. I have a team of knights with me." The other end of the phone counted, right?

Fergal eyed me curiously. "They let women be knights now? What's the world coming to?"

Because the world was in such a perfect state otherwise.

"Nobody *let* me. I don't need permission."

Okay, that wasn't strictly true. I had to pass a series of stringent tests to become a knight, but our most notable feature was that we were an all-female organization.

"I obviously hit a sore point."

"And I'm about to hit one of yours if you don't cooperate. You have something that belongs to my client and I'm here to reclaim it."

Fergal balled his hands into fists. "I won it fair and square."

"You didn't *win* anything. You drugged an entire table of players and stole it."

According to my client, Fergal served them all from the same pitcher of ale. My client thought it tasted bitter but before he could comment, he blacked out. When he lifted his head off the table an hour later, Fergal was gone and so was my client's jar of honey.

Fergal spat on the floor of the tunnel. "Prove it."

"I don't have to."

Fergal smacked the dog's backside. "Mongrel, take care of this girl."

Three heads growled again. So far Mongrel was all bark and no bite, which suited me fine.

"Did you even bring a weapon? How stupid can you be?"

If I were Fergal, I'd be more concerned by a knight who felt confident enough to venture down here without one.

I reached out with my mind and tried to make contact with the dog.

There you are, little lady.

Interesting. I expected three minds, but I only detected one. It seemed I was right to focus on the middle head. That was the control center. I touched the dog's mind and offered reassuring thoughts.

Little pig, little pig, let me come in.

The dog resisted.

I pushed a bit harder, prompting a snarl from all three heads.

"What are you doing, you lazy piece of shit? Attack!"

Fergal's demand had the opposite effect. The dog's mind squeaked opened and let me slither in.

Gotcha.

For her size, she wasn't too hard to win over. Probably because Fergal mistreated her. Those creatures were always easier to convert. Any port in a storm, bless her.

I transmitted my request.

"Mongrel, I said attack!" Fergal had no idea what was happening. I almost felt sorry for him.

Almost.

The left head turned first and growled at Fergal.

"Not me, you idiot," Fergal shouted.

Yes, call the multi-headed, fanged beast an idiot. That will help you.

The creature swung around and snapped three sets of jaws at Fergal.

"What did you do?" Fergal demanded.

"Mongrel, stay." The dog stilled and I held out my hand. "I'll take that jar of honey now."

Fergal's eyes bulged. "Even if I wanted to, I couldn't give it to you. I don't have it." He stumbled over his words, finally starting to comprehend the situation.

I clucked my tongue. "Fergal, aren't you in enough trouble already? Let's not drag this out."

"I sold it."

I resisted the urge to roll my eyes. Why, oh why did they insist on keeping up the charade when the jig was very clearly up?

I leaned down to address the creature. "Mongrel, when's the last time you ate?"

Three mouths began to salivate at the same time. Acidic slobber dripped from the jowls, forcing Fergal to take another step backward.

"Hold on," he said. "I'll get it."

I couldn't see past Fergal to know what he was getting, but every fiber of my being told me it wasn't what I came for.

Damn it, Fergal. I was trying to do this the easy way.

Metal flashed across the black backdrop.

Oh, well. I gave it my best shot. I would've preferred to handle this without help, but as I didn't have a weapon, I commandeered one.

"Mongrel, charge," I said.

The beast toppled Fergal. The sword flew to the right and clattered on the hard surface.

"Stay. No killing."

Mongrel kept her former owner pinned to the floor while I skirted them both. Nudging the sword out of his reach with my boot, I sauntered deeper into Fergal's lair. A few pots and pans. A canteen. A portable kerosene stove. A bedroll.

"Not much of a home," I said. Not that I was one to talk. My flat's most significant feature was indoor plumbing. Then again, we weren't vampires nor did we work for them. We didn't have the luxury of choice.

It was only when I shifted the bedroll that I found it. Jackpot. As the most valuable item in this mess, he'd wisely kept it hidden.

With the jar of honey in hand, I returned to the spot where Fergal was whimpering on the floor and rolling his head left to right to avoid the acidic spray of the beast's slobber.

"My client would like me to pass along a message. If you ever show your face at poker night again, you'll be leaving without your legs."

Fergal glowered at the creature on top of him. "I'll kill you for this, you worthless mutt."

I cut a sideways glance at the dog. Apparently I'd be leaving with more than a jar of golden honey. When possible, I released a creature I'd won over to my side. I had no interest in becoming the Snow White of Britannia City. I couldn't ignore Fergal's threat though. It wasn't fair to the dog.

I patted the creature's right head. "Come on, cutie. I'll get you a nice milk bone when we get out of here."

The beast stayed put.

"Sorry. Three milk bones."

The beast stepped off Fergal and trotted along beside me.

"Don't even think about grabbing your sword," I called without bothering to turn around.

I made my way to the exit with my new companion. "I have to ask—how do you maintain your balance with those heads?"

Three heads shifted to look at me. Impressive physiology happening there.

"I can't call you Mongrel," I said. "It's a terrible word to call anyone."

On the other hand, I didn't have a right to name her and I couldn't keep her. I felt torn. My flat wasn't big enough to accommodate a creature of her size, but if I released her now, she'd likely return to the tunnel if only because she was accustomed to it. If that happened, Fergal would make good on his threat. I couldn't risk it.

"Come on. I'll find you a temporary place to stay." I strode up the frozen escalator steps that led to the surface. "I bet you've never been to the Circus."

2

Thanks to well-preserved buildings and its close proximity to other sections of the city, Piccadilly Circus was a busy part of Britannia City. A few heads turned as I crossed the junction with a three-headed dog trotting beside me. We were accustomed to monster sightings around here, but not necessarily accustomed to seeing them behave like canine companions.

I stopped at the security desk in the building known as the Pavilion. The Pavilion dated back to the 1850s and housed a music hall before it became a shopping arcade. It fell into ruin after the Great Eruption until the Knights of Boudica claimed it as their headquarters. We weren't the only knights in the city, but because we were the only organization that was all female, we were the last call for the desperate, the poor, and the discreet. We took the jobs nobody else wanted because nobody else wanted us. I wasn't sure when breasts became a determining factor in how well someone could wield a blade, but I recognized the valuable service we provided. People who hired us were lucky to have us.

The security guard took one look at me and shook her head. Treena was used to seeing me in one of three states: moody, bloody, or accompanied by a newfound companion.

I feigned ignorance. "What?"

"One day I expect to see a parade of rats behind you."

"No thanks. Not a fan of rodents."

"Maybe not, but I bet they're a fan of you." Treena studied my companion. "One lanyard or three for your guest?"

"Let's forgo the lanyard today. I guarantee she'll take an instant dislike to you if you try to put something around her neck."

Treena made a noncommittal sound and waved us through the warded gate.

The dog kept pace with me as I approached the hub. Our headquarters was mainly open-plan except for an office designated for private client meetings, a small kitchen, an armory, and, of course, the loo. I didn't love the spacious feel of the building, mainly because I preferred to keep to myself and the layout prevented me from hiding. I tended to get around that issue by not turning up at the office except when necessary. I met with clients in alternate locations and only returned to headquarters at times like this when I needed the assistance of the other knights and to complete paperwork. As much as I hated asking for help, the dog deserved the effort.

"Look who made a new friend." I moved aside and made a ta-da motion with my hands. A collective groan followed.

"Not another one," Minka complained. Minka Tarlock inherited the dark hair, bronze skin, and wide, brown eyes of her Asian father and the height and accurate nose of her Nordic mother. She specialized in spells, which was the primary reason she worked in a more administrative capacity. There was rarely time to complete a spell in the field, especially if the ingredients needed were scarce.

"Another what? I've never brought a Cerberus here before."

Minka gave me a pointed look. "You know what I mean."

Briar shuffled out from behind her desk. "I'll get the dog bed." Briar Niall was a shapeshifter known for her wild red hair, creamy complexion, and heart of gold. When you wanted a checklist, you went to Minka. When you wanted a sympathetic ear, you went to Briar.

"The bed won't be big enough for that," Minka said.

"*That* has a name," I announced. At least she would as soon as I came up with something better than Mongrel.

Minka folded her arms. "What is it then?" When I didn't answer straight away, she laughed. "I knew it. You have no idea what its name is."

"As it happens, I do know, but it's a terrible name and she's in need of a new one."

Briar offered her hand to the middle head, palm flat. "It's okay. We're all friends here."

"*All* might be overstating it slightly," Minka mumbled.

"Mind the slobber or you might lose a hand," I said.

Briar snatched her hand away. "Do you think each head should have a different name?"

"One name should do it," I said. "The center head controls the other two."

"Then three heads aren't really better than one," Minka commented.

"They are when your goal is to intimidate," Briar said, now patting the top of a head. Not so intimidating after all.

"Go on," I urged Minka. "There's still one head available."

She gave me a tight smile. "No thanks. I just washed my

hands." She regarded the dog. "I guess the name Cerberus is too on the nose for you."

Briar snorted. "That would be like naming a newborn Baby." She crouched down and moved her nose closer to the nose on the left. "Do you have an opinion?"

Minka elbowed me lightly. "Can't you tell what she's thinking?"

"Not exactly." My skill didn't work that way. I couldn't have a telepathic conversation with the dog. The communication was more abstract and guided by feelings, except with the animals with whom I shared a strong bond, like Barnaby.

"What about Hella?" Briar asked.

Minka scrunched her nose. "This is a pointless exercise. She doesn't need to name it. The monster will go straight back where she found it as soon as she releases it."

"Therein lies the problem." I told them about Fergal. "Trio needs to steer clear of a certain section of the city and find a new home."

Briar lit up. "Trio's a great name."

I smiled. "Right? It just popped out."

Minka groaned. "It can't steer clear of Edgware Road by staying here."

"I wasn't suggesting here, specifically."

Trio barked and wagged her tail. Okay, maybe *she* was suggesting here specifically.

Minka's expression grew more pinched by the second. "Let me guess. There's no space in your flat."

"Of course there's no space." I gave the dog a playful smack on the back. "Sniff around and see who appeals to you."

Minka quickly returned to the safety of her desk. She avoided animals the way most people avoided vampires. I was pretty sure half the reason I brought creatures to the Circus was to see her reaction. Life held so very few pleasures.

Trio pressed three noses to the floor and sniffed loudly.

"You're not wearing your uniform again." Minka didn't bother to disguise her annoyed tone. "I don't know how you manage to run around the city without catching a chill."

I pivoted to face her. "That's what you're choosing to focus on?"

"Yes, I choose to focus on the rules. I know that must seem ridiculous to you…"

"I follow the rules," I objected.

"That uniform is designed to keep you safe." Minka gestured to Briar's dark blue outfit.

"And yet here I am—safe as houses and no uniform," I said.

I wasn't against a uniform on principle. There was a lot to be said for protective gear, especially ours. The Knights of Boudica had taken great pains to acquire the fluid-like magical armor that protected us from the cold, absorbed shock, and was difficult to penetrate, and I appreciated their efforts. I disliked wearing the uniform because it identified me as a knight and I tried to avoid anything that identified me in a crowd or drew attention to me. I wanted to blend with the shadows, the way vampires once did. It was safer for me. Safer for everyone.

While we argued, Trio had wandered over to Stevie's desk and was currently trying to pull the drawer handle with her fangs.

"I told Stevie it would attract animals if she kept snacks in her drawer," Minka said.

The drawer popped open and three heads alternated

dipping into the stash because they couldn't all fit at the same time.

"Tell Stevie I'll replace everything," I said.

"You better," Minka said. "She won't be happy."

"Shouldn't have left her desk unmanned," I said.

Minka went back to her paperwork. "She went with Ione and Neera to shop for supplies."

"What kind of shopping requires three knights?"

"They wanted a tie-breaker in case of a disagreement," Briar explained.

"Where's Kami?" I asked. She was the best option for dealing with Trio.

"Speak of the devil and I shall appear in his stead."

I spun around to see my friend limping toward us. Kamikaze Marwin was a tough, stocky blonde with a tongue that matched the sharpness of her blade. We met when we were both sixteen and orphaned. We lost contact for a few years when she left the city, but she made a point of finding me when she returned. We joined the Knights of Boudica together.

Minka rushed forward and yelled for Briar.

The shapeshifter vacated her chair. "I'm right here. I can see her."

"I'm fine," Kami insisted, nostrils flaring.

"You're limping," Minka said.

"Exactly. When I crawl in here on my belly because my legs are broken or missing, then you can call the resident healer."

Briar gave a slight bow of acknowledgment and backed away.

"How are you injured?" I asked. "You were supposed to be recuperating from yesterday."

"Sorry we can't all be part-Amazon and impervious to

injury," she griped.

I popped a hand on my hip. "I'm neither of those things and you know it." I was only five-nine, hardly Amazonian height, and I'd racked up enough injuries in my early days as a knight to earn the nickname Gash, which quickly fell out of favor when I threatened bodily harm.

Kami dragged herself to the nearest chair and sat. "It's a funny story I'll share when I'm in a better mood."

"I guess this isn't the ideal time to ask for a favor," I said.

Kami flicked her gaze to the beast currently devouring a bag of pretzels. "I don't suppose your favor involves three heads and an Olympic-Sized pool of acidic slobber."

I clasped my hands in front of me. "Speaking of funny stories…"

Kami raised a hand. "Save it. She's cute. I'll take her."

"I owe you one." I whistled and Trio trotted over to us. "Trio, this is your new friend, Kami. She's going to take good care of you."

Kami grunted. "Don't expect a warm bed and hot food. London only means that I'll introduce you to some other friendly critters who know where the good hunting is and you can roam the streets together."

There was safety in numbers even for a beast like Trio. At the very least it would save her from getting commandeered by a man like Fergal again.

"Now that the dog's sorted, I'll see you all later."

Minka frowned. "Where are you going?"

"I have to drop off the booty to our client so we get paid and then I have a meeting."

Minka glanced at her desk. "I don't have anything on the schedule."

"Because I didn't tell you about it."

Minka moaned her exasperation. "That's not how we do things, London."

"No, but it's how I do things." The meeting had been scheduled by Mack Quaid, a knight from one of the more acceptable banners.

"You need to tell me when you're moonlighting so I can make a note of it." Moonlighting was permissible under the rules, but Minka was overly obsessed with documentation in my opinion.

"I don't know yet if I am. Depends on the job."

Minka fixed me with an insistent stare. "But you'll let me know as soon as you decide?"

"Of course."

"She's lying," Kami said, flashing me a mischievous smile. Payback for ditching her with Trio, it seemed.

I smiled back. "Briar, I think Kami's in more pain than she's letting on. You might want to have her strip down and take a hot bath whether she wants to or not. She can be her own worst enemy."

Kami detested baths. For Kami, baths were akin to stewing in your own filth.

Briar headed toward Kami with a determined set of her jaw. "Stop putting on a brave face and let me heal you. It's one of my strengths, remember?"

"Oh, I remember," Kami replied. "I'm still recovering from yesterday's healing session."

Winking at Kami, I gave Trio a final pat on all three heads and exited the Circus.

THERE WERE dive bars in the city and then there was Hole, which was a pretty apt description. The owner was a portly werewolf named George who stored a cache of weapons under the counter behind a red and white gingham curtain.

Ask me how I know.

George lifted his chin in greeting. He knew better than to call anyone's name across the room. Nobody came here to be greeted like a member of the family. They came here to drink and stay lost. I came here to meet the clients sent to me by Mack.

I barely made it through the door when I felt the back of my neck tingle. A quick scan of the room told me which one he was. Terrific. George had seated a vampire in the booth where I was supposed to meet my client. I didn't blame George for letting him sit there. Nobody wanted to make trouble with a vampire. It was too easy to get your pub shut down for some bullshit violation.

All the other high-backed booths were taken and I needed the privacy. I'd have to tread carefully.

I sauntered over to the booth to greet the hooded figure who sat hunched over the table. A half-filled glass of whisky rested close to his hand. Hole was a cheap place and whisky was one of the most expensive offerings on the nonexistent menu.

"I hate to be the bearer of bad news, but this booth is taken. There are plenty of stools at the bar and I have it on good authority that George doesn't bite."

"All shifters bite. It's a matter of when, not if," the hooded figure responded in a deep, surprisingly smooth voice.

I slid into the seat across from him and folded my hands on the table. "That's a pretty bold assertion—and pretty rude considering you're sitting in George's pub."

My gaze raked over him, trying to get a read on the mysterious stranger. I didn't want to push too hard and cause a scene. He reeked of danger the way the underground tunnels reeked of stale fear.

"Listen, I'm supposed to meet a client here and if he sees you and I chatting away like old friends, he's going to find someone else to hire, which would be bad for business."

"Business? Are you a lady of the night?"

I snorted. "Haven't you heard? There's an eternal eclipse. We're all ladies of the night now."

"And I'm your client." He slipped off the hood and two green eyes shone back at me, hard and bright like two emeralds. Dark blond hair covered his head in soft waves. His face had the kind of rugged handsomeness that drew the attention of everyone with functional eyesight. Even now, with his hood lowered, I felt the eyes of every patron on us. On him. They weren't staring at a vampire in a place he didn't belong. They were staring at the finest male specimen they'd ever seen. Like me, they were equal parts terrified and awestruck.

I sat perfectly still and tried not to react. I'd never seen a vampire in Hole before, which was one of the reasons I preferred this place, but there was a first time for everything.

I maintained a casual air. "As I said, you've got the wrong booth."

"And as I said, I'm your client."

There was no way a vampire wanted to hire someone like me. This had to be a mistake.

"Who sent you?"

His mouth quirked, drawing my attention to it. With lips like his, you barely noticed the fangs.

"I assure you, I'm quite certain you're the one I'm meant to meet."

I allowed a lazy smile to caress my lips. "When you say it like that, you make it sound like fate."

He pinned me with those two glittering gems. "Do you believe in fate?"

The lump in my throat grew larger and harder to swallow. "Tell me who arranged this meeting and we can proceed."

"Mack Quaid, Knight of the First Order."

Holy hellfire. Mack really did send me a vampire. I was going to throttle him. Better yet, I would introduce him to my new friend Trio. I'd teach her how to fetch a ball first and then let the dog loose on Mack.

"What's your name?" the vampire asked, smooth and soft, like he was lulling me to sleep after an intense and exhausting session of bedroom activity.

"You first."

His mouth twitched. "Lincoln."

"London."

He grunted. "London? Interesting choice."

"My mother was a history buff. She liked to say the past is full of warning signs. It's helpful to read them."

"Wise woman. And you're a Knight of Boudica?"

How much had Mack told him about me? "Does it matter?"

"I asked for the best."

"If you want the best, there are more official channels you could've taken."

Ignoring me, he nodded to George. "Care for a drink before we begin?"

"Water for me, thank you."

George knew what to serve me. Even if someone ordered me a vodka tonic, I was to be given a glass of water. A woman couldn't be too careful and I was always careful. Then again, a man like Lincoln could make a girl throw caution to the wind. Too bad he was a vampire.

A server appeared with a glass of water for me and another whisky for my client. She lingered for a moment, her gaze fixed on him as though hoping for some kind of acknowledgement.

"That will be all," he finally said. The dismissal was firm, like the hint of muscle that strained beneath his cloak.

The server's mouth turned down at the corners and she scuttled away.

What was she hoping for? A brief moment of plug and play on the table?

"Why don't you tell me what you want?" The sooner I extracted the information, the sooner I could get out of here and far away from him. The close proximity to a vampire was making me deeply uncomfortable. And my primal reaction to him didn't help.

His finger circled the rim of the glass. "I need you to recover something for me."

I leaned against the back of the booth. "I'll need a little more information than 'something.'"

"Do you treat all your clients with the same kind of irreverence or am I special?"

Special didn't even begin to cover it. "As you can imagine, I can't track something without knowing what it is. At the very least, I need a description and where you last saw it. You know, the basics."

What could a vampire possibly need someone like me to track? They had the best knights at their disposal. Official ones like Mack, yet the vampire was seated across from me in need of my help. Something didn't add up.

His penetrating gaze unsettled me. "You seem...uncomfortable. Is anything the matter? If it's the location, we can meet elsewhere. I was told this was your preferred meeting place." He surveyed the room. "Rather clandestine."

I had a bad habit of wearing my feelings on my face. I hid my species, yet I couldn't hide my dismay or suspicion. You'd think after thirty years, I'd be better at that.

I tore my gaze away and snapped to attention.

Whatever the job was, I couldn't do it. I avoided vampires at all costs and now here I was, sharing a table with one of the deadly bloodsuckers.

No thanks.

I slipped out of the booth and rose to my feet. "Sorry. Mack was mistaken. I don't have room in the schedule."

He looked at me with a mixture of curiosity and...respect?

"I think what you really mean to say is you won't work for a vampire."

"I couldn't possibly say that."

His mouth split in an amused grin. "Only because you're worried about repercussions, not because it isn't true."

"I'm sorry I wasted your time, but you'll have to find someone else."

Lightning-fast, he reached out and grabbed my hand. The movement was so swift and unexpected that I nearly drew my dagger on instinct. I was relieved to have exercised self-control. Pulling a weapon on a vampire in a public place was madness.

"And what if I don't want anyone else?" he asked in a low voice that promised so much more than a paycheck.

Nice try, sexy beast, but no dice. I extracted my hand from his firm grip. "As I said, my dance card is currently full. You'll have to seek another partner."

There was nothing else I could say that wouldn't get me in water hot enough to boil my skin, so I exercised the only option left to me.

I walked out.

3

I left Hole just as the streetlights dimmed to indicate nighttime. I headed straight for the headquarters of the Knights of the First Order. Despite the hour, I knew Mack would be there and he had a lot of explaining to do. He didn't know my secret, of course, but he knew how our banner felt about vampires. Before the Eternal Night began, no one knew vampires even existed. They still lived in the shadows—until those shadows extended across the globe and became the norm. Humans weren't designed to live in a world without sunlight, but vampires were. The rise of vampires prompted shapeshifters and magic users to emerge from hiding as well, but their abilities proved no match for the strength of bloodsuckers in a sunless world. Humans were pushed toward the bottom of the food chain, forced to register as potential blood donors at government tribute centers. Under House Lewis, the system was set up as a lottery, much like jury duty.

I strode through Covent Garden and replayed the meeting in my mind. Minka would have a coronary if she knew I turned down a vampire. She'd worry about repercussions for the banner if he decided to file a complaint. We didn't want to court the negative attention of vampires. They could make life very difficult for a small operation like ours. We could lose our license to use magic, which would render us useless and unemployed. My infrequent meals would become even more so. Still, better hungry than dead.

Halfway through Covent Garden I passed one of the largest memorials in the city. A team of artists had created a ring of ten volcanoes to commemorate the Great Eruption. Each one was identified by a small plaque. La Garita Caldera that spanned Colorado, Utah, and Nevada in the United States. Lake Toba in North Sumatra. Cerro Guacha, a Miocene caldera in southwestern Bolivia. Yellowstone Caldera in Wyoming in the United States. Lake Taupo on what was once the North Island of New Zealand. Cerro Galán in Argentina. Island Park Caldera, one of the world's largest calderas that crossed the borders of Idaho and Wyoming in the United States. Vilama, the Miocene caldera in Bolivia and Argentina. La Pacana, the Miocene age caldera in Chile. Pastos Grandes, the caldera and crater lake in Bolivia. Scientists had reassured people for decades that they had nothing to fear from the supervolcanoes.

Scientists were wrong.

Not that there was much they could've done to prevent the aftermath. Once the cloud of ash expanded to coat the earth's atmosphere, there was a period of death and destruction as the world struggled to adjust to the new normal. The vampires saw their opportunity and seized it with both fangs. They took control, using witches and wizards to create a magical infrastructure that kept plants alive and stopped mass extinction. They had an ulterior motive, of course. With human blood as their primary food source, they were desperate to preserve it. To do that successfully, they had to keep the human population fed and thriving, hence the use of electricity to replicate day and night, among other things. Apparently humans tasted better when they weren't in a constant state of distress. I preferred not to think about it in greater detail.

I noticed someone had vandalized the memorial of Vilama by writing 'freedom' in yellow spray paint. I wasn't sure I agreed with the sentiment. Yes, South America was one continent the vampires failed to control, but only because they abandoned it to the monsters. The vampires in North America employed a team of wizards and witches that worked around the clock to provide a line of defense at the southern and western borders. European and Asian Houses were able to accumulate more power because they didn't have to expend their energy defending their borders from an entire continent of monsters or repairing mass destruction. There'd been other kinds of destruction as a result of the Eternal Night, but not on the scale of what the Americas and Australasia had faced. Places like New Zealand and Indonesia no longer existed, claimed by lava. One of the benefits of Lake Taupo's location, though, was that most of the monsters that emerged from that caldera failed to survive. Unless they could swim or fly, they were doomed from the moment they were spat into the realm.

I made a pitstop at the twenty-four-hour bakery and continued to Tavistock Street where the Knights of the First Order enjoyed a refurbished period property with meeting rooms and individual offices. Two columns flanked the doorway and over the entrance was a carving of the sun. Both the carving itself and its subject were remnants of the past. There were still those who remembered sunlight, although their numbers dwindled year after year. Witches and wizards enjoyed longer lifespans than most, but many of them worked themselves to the breaking point as a key part of the vampires' infrastructure. Shapeshifters lived longer under ideal circumstances, but their need for massive quantities of food meant they didn't often live to their full potential unless they were part of a powerful pack. The thriving packs tended to be those that struck deals with vampires and offered their brute strength in areas like security, building, and agriculture.

I stopped at the door to greet the security guard, Lawrence.

"Anything in that bag for me?" he asked.

I gave him the bag from the bakery. "You know my mother raised me right. Is he in?"

"Where else would he be?"

I ticked off the options on my fingers. "Home with his wife. Working in the field. Trapped under a well-fed manticore."

Lawrence chuckled. "Go ahead up."

I crossed the threshold and took a moment to admire the few period features that had been retained. The brass light fixtures were a smart choice. Thanks to my mother, I knew that brass was easy to maintain and worth preserving, not a fact that many building owners seemed to know. She'd impressed upon me the importance of history. No matter how long ago and inconsequential a story or a detail seemed, there was always the potential to learn from it. I once complained about having to memorize passages about the Boston Tea Party in the United States. What could someone in Britannia City hope to gain from a story about angry human colonists dumping tea into a harbor an ocean away as an act of rebellion? My mother told me to pretend King George III was a vampire and then decide how irrelevant it was. I saw her point. It was also heartening to learn the colonists eventually won their war. I chose to ignore the fact that their victory was short-lived in the grand scheme of the universe. Hope, like the night, was eternal.

I took the staircase to the second floor. Very few knights would be here now. Knights of the First Order worked what some referred to as 'bank hours.' Not Mack. He was a workaholic. Probably one of the reasons we got along.

Well, we weren't going to get along tonight. I was too pissed off. By the time I arrived at his office, I'd worked myself into a fury.

"Are you out of your mind?" I towered over Mack's desk with my arms tightly folded and anger simmering just below the surface. Poke a hole in my skin right now and steam would seep out.

Mack glanced up at me, unconcerned. His broad shoulders and skill with a blade made him a popular knight. A round, cheerful face with ruddy cheeks regardless of alcohol intake and a dry sense of humor made him popular at the pub. Today he wore business casual attire instead of magical armor. The collared white shirt made him look more like an accountant than a knight.

"Did you even bother to stop at security?" he asked.

"Sure. I gave Lawrence a scone as I passed by. He seemed grateful. I don't think you pay him enough."

Mack shook his head. "I'll need to have a talk with him about the definition of security."

"No one bearing scones can possibly be a threat. It's an unwritten law."

He looked at me expectantly. "Where's my scone?"

"You don't deserve a scone." My face hardened. "Not after the little mix-up with the vampire...And please tell me it *was* a mix-up."

Mack's expression told a different story. "It's a job, isn't it?

I thought you wanted those. This one even paid more." He paused. "*A lot* more."

"What I want is to have nothing to do with vampires and you sat me across from one like we were on a date." I eyed his desk to see if there were a few loose sheets of paper I could scatter around to punctuate my displeasure, but Mack was too tidy for that.

He cocked an eyebrow. "That attractive, huh?"

I straightened. "I didn't say that."

"You basically did. If he were old and fat, you wouldn't have used the date analogy. You'd have said something along the lines of 'like I was his steak dinner *and* his side of potatoes.'"

"That does sound like me, doesn't it?"

Mack smirked. "You have a way with analogies. One of the things I like about you."

"Finally. An admission that you like me rather than tolerate me."

Mack and I met three years ago on an assignment in Camden. It turned out we'd both been given the same job by the same client who wasn't confident that either one of us could perform to his satisfaction. I ended up bagging the beast and impressing Mack at the same time. He started sending overflow work my way, usually one that involved a specific set of skills. Of course I still had no idea why I was the best knight for the vampire's particular assignment. I'd have to quash my curiosity though. I didn't want to entertain any further thoughts of the vampire with his bright green eyes and corded muscle.

As I continued to stand at the desk glowering, an unpleasant realization occurred to me. "Why don't you know what he looks like? Please tell me it's one of those I'm-a-heterosexual-male-therefore-I have-no-clue-how-hot-other-guys-are situations."

Mack fell silent and reality slammed into my chest with both feet first.

"Holy hellfire. You didn't meet him in person first?" I balled my hand into a fist and fought the urge to punch his face. "You're supposed to vet everyone you send my way."

Mack suddenly found the grooves of his desk very interesting. "Trust me. He's on the level."

Leaning forward, I splayed my hands on his desk. "He's a vampire, Mack."

Mack grinned. "What gave it away? The smoldering good looks? The expensive clothes?"

Straightening, I folded my arms and glared at him. "The fangs." No need to tell Mack I had my own built-in vampire detector. Some secrets were meant to be kept.

Mack fiddled with a pen. "Truth be told I didn't know I was sending you to work for a vamp and it didn't occur to me to ask."

"There was a middleman?"

He nodded.

Strange. Why use a middleman? "Someone you trust, presumably."

Mack nodded. "When he sets me up with a job, I don't ask questions."

"Why send this one to me?"

"Because he asked for a specific set of skills and you were the best equipped for the job."

"What skills did he specify?"

Mack eyed me closely. "What does it matter? Sounds like you didn't take the job."

"Now you've got me curious." I settled in the chair opposite him and rested the heels of my boots on the edge of the desk.

"You know how it works. The information is confidential unless the job is yours."

"So now I'm out of a job *and* gossip?" I clucked my tongue. "Mack, you disappoint me."

Mack dragged a hand through his thinning brown hair. "You really walked out?"

"I really did."

"Shit."

"Don't worry. He won't blame you. I was clear about how I felt."

He grimaced. "How clear?"

I ignored the question. "I've got a hole in my schedule now. Got anything else for me that doesn't involve vampires?"

He expelled a breath. "I've got a job that's just come in from Perth. If you want it, it's yours."

I pulled a face.

Mack groaned. "Seriously? What's the problem with Perth?"

"His jobs always end with me doused in bodily fluids. I could spend forty-eight hours in the shower after a Perth job and still feel dirty."

Mack arched an eyebrow. "Do I want to know?"

"There was the dragon in Westminster that was terrorizing the people in a high-rise and someone shot its wing with a crossbow just as I arrived. Who happened to be standing below and got splashed with gooey dragon blood?" I pointed to myself. "That's right. This girl."

"But you like animals. They're kind of your thing."

"This one was one too angry to be won over and the people attacking it didn't help matters."

Mack tossed a file across the desk. "This one involves fluids too. There's a creature in the Serpentine terrifying families. Last week some kid went on a picnic with his family and almost lost a leg. Thankfully the parents pulled him out in time."

"Since when does Perth care about the safety of children?"

Mack shrugged. "You know how he is. He owns small companies that own smaller companies. There's a food stall in Hyde Park and whatever's in the water is hurting his business."

I flipped through the file. "Probably a kelpie."

"That's my theory." He tilted his head. "Can I make it official?"

I sighed. "Fine." I really did need the money and a kelpie wouldn't pose too much of a challenge.

He winked. "Don't say I never gave you anything."

"As long as you don't give me a communicable disease." All these foreign fluids couldn't be good for my system.

"Not possible if you keep turning down my dinner invitations."

I smiled. It was a running joke between us that he wanted to date me and I perpetually rejected him. The truth was Mack was happily married to Juanita, but he didn't want that fact to be common knowledge. In our line of work, loved ones became a target for a vengeful mark. Loved ones also made us vulnerable. The closest I was willing to get to love were my animal companions.

Returning to my feet, I tucked the file under my arm. "I'll let you know when it's done."

Mack flipped his pen in the air and caught it. "And next time bring me a scone too."

4

A row of streetlights lined the path to the lake in Hyde Park. It was a good effort, but the faint glow didn't do much to cut through the gloom in an area like this. Electricity could only do so much and frequent power surges resulted in blackouts. Crime was rampant in certain parts of the city and most residents were smart enough to travel in groups, even for leisurely outings like a picnic. You didn't stop living your life. You simply crossed your fingers and hoped for the best. Sometimes people got lucky, like the boy who escaped. Sometimes they didn't.

My mother once told me there was a brief period of time when the park was devoid of life. When the Eternal Night began, people cleared out of the city in droves. For some reason they felt safer in the countryside, which turned out to be a false sense of security.

When the dust literally settled, people thought it was over—that soon life would return to normal, but it was only the beginning. The supervolcanoes had spewed more than ash when they erupted. Soon creatures believed only to exist in storybooks crawled out of the earth's belly. It was as though the goddess Gaia gave birth to the Titans all over again. It wasn't until the monsters made their way here from their respective birthplaces that the true horror sank in.

Slowly the population became acclimated and adjusted to the new normal. Signs of life returned to the city and eventually people grew accustomed to perpetual darkness. They even resumed leisure activities, albeit with a heightened sense of awareness. If you wanted to picnic and go for a swim, you had to know there was a chance you wouldn't be alone in the water.

Despite the afternoon hour, there was no sign of merrymakers or business operators. Word must've gotten out that Hyde Park had a monster problem. No wonder Perth was desperate.

Finally the lake came into view. The Serpentine was manmade, created in 1730 by Queen Caroline. It covered forty acres of land between Hyde Park and what was once Kensington Gardens. I spent an inordinate amount of time as a child admiring books in the library that featured gardens. My mother helped fuel that particular obsession. Gardens were a thing of the past unless you were a royal vampire. House Lewis, the ruling vampire family that controlled most of England, also controlled the growth of plants in the region. The House employed a team of witches and wizards whose sole job consisted of using magic to grow plants. Not all magic users possessed the same type of magic, so House Lewis made sure to hire employees with a variety of abilities. Witches with earth magic or water magic worked alongside wizards proficient in spells. The results were closely guarded and highly valuable.

A closer review of the file from Mack made me rethink the kelpie theory. Based on the marks on the boy's leg and the witness testimony, my money was now on a selkie.

Vampires weren't particularly interested in preventing death by selkie, so it fell to organizations like ours to work on behalf of a client—and that client was usually motived by money rather than altruism, as was the case with Perth. That wasn't to say vampires did nothing. Bodies of water in the city were treated by magic on a regular basis to keep out harmful bacteria and parasites. Unfortunately the magic wasn't powerful enough to keep out the kind of creatures that preyed on people.

I positioned myself at the water's edge and peered at the lake. There were no obvious signs of life. Ducks and swans that once swam across the Serpentine had been eaten and replaced by creatures of the deep years ago.

"Rise and shine, sweetness. You've got company!"

No response.

Selkies weren't always considered dangerous. In fact, there was a time when they were viewed as downright docile. Seals in the water and women on land. No interest in eating or drowning anyone. But like so many things in the world, that changed with the coming of the Eternal Night. Many modern selkies were opportunistic hunters that had no qualms about dragging children to their doom. Far less civilized than vampire-run tribute centers.

Despite their violent evolution, selkies weren't high on my personal list of big bad threats. I'd dispatched more than I cared to count. The last one was causing trouble in the sewer system of all places. Yet another job that required a deep scrub afterward. Despite my track record, you could never be too careful when dealing with a creature in the wild. I had no idea when this selkie's last meal was. Empty bellies made poor choices.

I scanned the lake and noted the water rippling across the middle. The air around me was perfectly still.

Found you.

I clapped my hands. "Here, selkie selkie selkie."

The water rippled closer to me and then spread itself flat.

Hmm. Someone was playing hard to get.

Good thing I came prepared. I dug my fingers into my right pocket and tossed a handful of breadcrumbs in the water. The crumbs floated on the surface of the water, untouched.

"Not a fan of carbs. Totally understand."

I reached into my left pocket and produced a knotted bag filled with chunks of raw meat.

Like I said, I came prepared.

I opened the bag as close to shore as I could manage without dumping the meat on land. Droplets of blood splattered on the water. Not enough to draw a vampire's interest, but enough to lure the selkie.

I emptied the bag of its contents. That ought to do it.

Less than a minute later a head surfaced. The selkie had opted for her female form. Good. That made communication easier.

I waved. "Hey, friend."

She swam toward me with all the grace you'd expect from a water-based monster. Long, reddish-orange hair fanned out behind her and her alabaster skin glistened in the dim light.

"Care for a swim?" Like many of her species, her voice had a singsong quality to it.

"No thanks." I produced the badge that identified me as a knight. "I'm London Hayes and I'm here as a Knight of Boudica to officially request your evacuation from these waters."

The selkie moved to float on her back, revealing small

breasts and a flat torso. Her bottom half was gray and slick like a seal.

"Too bad. I'm partial to these waters," the selkie protested.

"Your personal preference is irrelevant. As I said, this is an official request."

Her eyes narrowed but remained focused on the dark sky above. "This lake is public property. I have the same right to be here as everyone else."

"Only when you don't break the rules, which you did when you attacked a boy. He wasn't thrown to you as an offering. He was on a picnic with his family."

She turned her head to peer at me. "You can't prove it was me."

"Don't have to. I'm a knight, not an adjudicator."

The selkie pursed her full lips. "It's discriminatory."

I folded my arms. "What is?"

"Children are nutritious. All that baby fat is delicious."

I ignored the unpleasant image that sprang to mind. "I don't make the rules."

The selkie spat a fountain of water high in the air. "What do vampires care about the safety of human children? They see them as a source of food the same as I do."

"There are two problems with that statement. One is that the kid you tried to eat was a werewolf not a human. Two is the assumption that vampires share food."

The rules that protected residents weren't necessarily in place for the benefit of humans. There were, however, times like this when they helped me do my job. Even Perth didn't care much about one werewolf child. He did, however, care very much about his bottom line. If this selkie continued to terrorize people, park businesses would suffer.

Her breasts and torso disappeared beneath the surface

of the water as she mulled over my argument. "The vampires sent you?"

"Yes," I lied.

"Meh. Don't care. I'm staying." She submerged her head, which was the selfie equivalent of *na-na, I can't hear you*.

Great. Of all the selkies in all the lakes, I had to get the one with the attitude of a spoiled teenager.

I waited and counted to ten in my head. No sign of her.

The easy way was officially off the table. Good thing my uniform was waterproof. Minka would be proud of me for wearing it.

"If I have to step foot in this cold water, you're going to regret your contrary attitude," I called.

The water remained still.

Kicking off my boots, I removed my sheath and dropped my weapons on the shore. They were no use in the lake. Magic underwater wasn't impossible, but there was more resistance. I'd have to take that into account.

I waded in and immediately shivered. Too bad the uniform didn't cover my feet. I dove headfirst as soon as I reached hip level. I was a strong swimmer thanks to youthful adventures I'd rather not have experienced. They made me a better knight though.

My eyes burned underwater. I scanned the murky depths of the lake for any sign of the selkie. She had the advantage of living here and would know the terrain.

But I had the advantage of magic.

I tapped into the minds of the aquatic life around me to see whether I could garner any local support. Blank minds abounded in Hyde Park. Great.

Before I could widen my range, something wrapped around my ankle and yanked me downward. I bent sideways for a glimpse of my captor, expecting to see the selkie.

Instead I saw a scaly sea serpent whose bottom half was currently curled around my ankle.

The selkie had minions.

Another sea serpent appeared to the left of me and twined its body around my arm.

I reached for its mind, but there was nothing firm to latch onto. The selkie must've had her own method of controlling them. If she were a siren, I could make an educated guess, but selkies were a different species. A siren could lure you to your death with an enticing song. A selkie's vocal skills were limited to a singsong voice.

I kicked and punched in an effort to loosen the serpents' grip. My resistance only made them tighten their hold on me. Any tighter and they'd cut off my circulation. I'd lose half my limbs.

Like my mother, I had elemental magic, although I didn't have a reason to use powerful water magic very often. My needs were more basic, like filtering my drinking water so I could hydrate without falling ill.

I focused on the water until I felt a connection form. The sensation was like fitting a key into a lock and twisting until you felt that satisfying click. As soon as I felt the click, I pushed the water down and around—down and around—until a small water cyclone formed and caught the serpents in its spiral. They'd been so focused on securing me that they hadn't noticed the aberration.

I slipped free and propelled myself to the surface for a gasp of air. I could hold my breath under water longer than any human I knew, but I didn't have gills.

My head crested the water and two serpent heads bobbed up next to me less than a minute later. I'd have to work on my water skills. As my mother would've said, this was what happened when I didn't practice.

"We meet again," I told the serpents. "Not to worry. I can do this with one hand tied behind my back."

Two more serpent heads broke the surface.

"Okay. I might need both hands." And both legs. Treading water was great for exercise but not so great when you were trying to conjure magic. It was akin to trying to pat your head and rub your belly at the same time.

If I spent too much energy dealing with the serpents, I'd have to regroup before I handled the selkie or I'd end up causing more harm than good. Some magic users felt depleted after expending too much energy. I was the opposite.

I became dangerous.

Despite my effort to remain calm, my body betrayed me, switching to high alert.

My magic flared. *No, no, no.*

Most magic users had it easy. They had one set of skills like telepathy or power over water, which they mastered and then controlled with the same effort they employed for breathing and sleeping.

As I discovered early on, I was not that kind of magic user.

On the one hand, I was fortunate because I possessed multiple skills. On the other hand, I sucked because I possessed multiple skills. Ever hear that phrase Jack of all trades, master of none? Pretty sure that was written about me.

My magic swirled inside me like a tempest that only calmed when I expelled some of it. It was exhausting to carry around with me all day every day. As a child, magic had a tendency to overwhelm me and my mother devised coping strategies to keep it contained. It couldn't have been easy for her—my mother's magic wasn't like mine. Hers wasn't as straightforward as other witches and wizards we knew, but it wasn't the illogical mess that mine was.

My mother did everything she could to make me more comfortable. She didn't want my magic to leak at an inopportune moment. Illegal use of magic risked getting the attention of vampires which, in turn, risked revealing what I was.

Losing control of my magic was a death sentence.

I had to deal with the serpents swiftly so I could find the selkie. Why did she have to be so stubborn? There was an entire ocean awaiting her. Then again, there were very few nutritious children in the middle of the Atlantic.

I made one final effort to reach their minds. Nope. Nada. Some creatures just weren't sentient enough to get them to submit. I'd have to resort to a different type of magic.

All four serpents cut a line through the water toward me at the same time. Time for a minor bit of spell magic.

"Levitas."

My body lifted out of the water as though pulled by an invisible giant hand. I hovered a foot above the water and watched as the serpents undulated beneath me, their scaly black bodies crisscrossing in the water. Levitation wasn't my strong suit and I knew I could only hold this pose for less than a minute.

Perched on a rock in the middle of the lake was the selkie. Smiling, she waved and dove into the water.

This was embarrassing. Outsmarted by a common selkie. Not my best showing.

I released a bit more magic, careful not to allow too much to spill out. Other than Kami, the banner had no idea how hard it was for me to control my magic. If they suspected that I was a loose cannon, I'd be ejected from the knighthood faster than you can say Boudica. It didn't matter how much they needed my skills, if I was a security risk to the group, I was out. Just one more reason to hide my true self. It was a wonder I managed to form relationships with anyone at all.

I had to nip this in the bud. As the levitation spell expired, I dropped back to the water and *pushed*. The muscles in my neck strained as I fought to contain the rest of my magic. The water parted, creating an oblong gap for me to land in and dividing the serpents just shy of six feet on either side of the lake bottom. Landing on solid ground, I extended both arms and grabbed the two closest serpents by the neck, wrenching them from the water. I spun them as dual lassos until they collided in front of me. I reached for the other two serpents, but they'd wisely disappeared.

The selkie poked her head through the curtain of water and bared her teeth, taunting me. I caught a glimpse of small, sharp teeth before she closed her mouth and said, "Catch me if you can."

I wasn't in the mood for games. I was in the mood to go home and shower and buy a hot meal with the money I earned today.

The selkie was an obstacle to my simple yet pleasant future.

"I don't want to hurt you," I yelled. *But I will if I have to*.

Preparing my escape route, I opened a path to shore. It wasn't very far, but I was a faster runner than swimmer and who knew what other monsters lurked in the lake? At this point, I would've roused every single one of them.

The selkie must've been watching me from the depths of the water because she emerged in human form and landed behind me on the path. She was smarter than I gave her credit for.

She used her human foot to kick me squarely in the

kidneys. I pitched forward and lost my control on the water. It flooded the path and crashed against me. The selkie took the opportunity to switch her bottom half back to seal form. Before I recovered from her unexpected maneuver, I felt sharp teeth prick my skin.

Ouch!

I elbowed her in the face. Even in the murk, I could see her eyes blaze with anger. I focused, intending to create another whirlpool around the selkie to isolate her. The water began to churn and I released a bit more magic. I was so intent on creating the whirlpool that I failed to notice a solid object skim the surface above our heads. A strong arm plunged into the water and grabbed the selkie by her long hair, ejecting her from the lake.

What the hell?

I shot to the surface in time to see a vampire break the selkie's neck. He flung her back into the lake and I watched in silent fury as she sank to the bottom.

"What do you think you're doing?" I yelled.

"What does it look like? Helping you."

"I didn't need your help. I had it under control!" It took me a moment to realize it was the vampire from Hole standing on a paddleboard. "You!"

He bowed with a flourish. "You're welcome."

"Are you kidding me? Where did you even get a paddleboard? None of the stalls are open."

"I'm resourceful."

I pulled myself on the paddleboard and tried to shove him in the water.

He appeared both shocked and amused by the gesture. "You'll have to put a bit more muscle into it if you intend to move me."

I frowned and pushed again, this time even harder. Even

balanced on a board, he was like a brick wall. Impossible to move.

He laughed like I'd told him a funny joke. "You were in trouble and I rescued you."

"It was under control," I ground out.

He gave the lake a speculative glance. "Interesting. From my perspective, it looked like you were about to be drowned by a selkie. She'd definitely gained the upper hand."

"It wasn't anything I couldn't handle." I balanced on the edge of the board and debated whether to swim back to shore.

He picked up the paddle and dipped the end in the water. "You must be tired after your fierce battle. Care for a lift to shore?"

My jaw tightened. Who did this guy think he was?

"Why are you here? Are you stalking me?" A vampire trailing after me in a deserted park? I couldn't let that threat go unchallenged.

"Rein in your ego. I wasn't stalking you." He seemed to want to laugh.

I'll show you something funny. In one swift move, I sliced my leg underneath his feet and knocked him backward. Incredibly, he managed to stay on the board. I launched myself on top of him and kneeled on his neck with as much force as I could muster.

"Truce," he choked out. The board rocked side to side as a gust of wind created waves.

"You would say that, wouldn't you?"

He raised his hands in acquiescence. "I'm here on behalf of House Lewis."

I froze. "What was that?"

"House. Lewis. I'm Prince Callan."

Multiple curse words strained to pass my lips, but I suppressed them.

Prince Callan. House Lewis.

He took advantage of my shock and flipped me on my back. The back of my head slammed against the board and I tasted blood in my mouth. Stupid tongue always getting in the way. In more ways than one.

The board rocked again and he caught the paddle before it slid into the water.

"You said your name was Lincoln!"

"I lied. I'm Prince Callan and I'm here on royal business."

"I know who you are," I said through gritted teeth.

Everybody knew the name Prince Callan, otherwise known as the Demon of House Duncan, the Highland Reckoning, and the Lord of Shadows. He wasn't the natural son of the king and queen of House Lewis. He'd been delivered as a hostage and a show of good faith when Houses Lewis and Duncan signed a peace treaty twenty years ago. He also single-handedly brought the city of Birmingham to its knees during his father's march to Britannia City in one of the most violent battles between the Houses' respective armies. He was twelve at the time.

"Good, if you know who I am, then you know what I can do to you." His gaze lingered on my lips and I felt my body tense in response. He was talking about killing me, right? The way his eyes were locked on my face instead of my neck...Those fangs promised I'd be screaming—whether from pleasure or pain, I wasn't sure.

I wriggled out from under him and he shifted his weight to release me. I couldn't let him know that I could've done a lot more damage to him than he realized.

"Let's try this again," I said. I held out my hand for the paddle.

He eyed me warily. "You won't use it as a weapon?"

"No, I'm going to paddle us to shore. While I do that hard labor, you can tell me why you're following me."

"I've been watching you."

I cut a glance at him as I pushed us through the water. "Not at all creepy."

"You've impressed me."

Fear pricked my skin. How much did he see? I racked my brain for all the magic I performed. Was there anything that could've given me away? I didn't think so.

I raised my chin a fraction. "I have a license to perform magic."

"Oh I know. And I'm more convinced than ever you're the right one for the job."

"The job you offered me and I already turned down? That job?"

A smile tugged at the corners of his mouth. "Yes. That job."

"There are dozens of knights to choose from. Try one of them." I turned away and continued paddling. Almost to shore.

"I want you."

My heart beat rapidly at the sound of his velvety voice telling me, of all things, that he wanted me. My lips parted but no sound came out.

"Need help loosening your tongue? I might know a few tricks."

I bet. "I'm good, thanks."

"I'd like to extend an invitation to the official residence of House Lewis to discuss the matter in greater detail."

My head jerked toward him. "You mean the palace?"

The royal family-owned multiple residences throughout the city as well as the countryside.

"Do you know it?"

"Hard to miss." It was a sprawling building called Buckingham Palace that once served as the official administrative residence of the House of Windsor, the last royal human family before the Eternal Night began.

"Good, then I don't need to give you the address."

Only a few more feet to shore and my weapons. "And what if I don't show?"

"You will be well-compensated."

The board slid onto solid ground and I caught sight of my sheath exactly where I left it. I stepped off the board and handed him the paddle.

"Maybe money isn't the only thing that motivates me. I'd like to know more now before I waste my time."

His eyes narrowed. "You will know more when I choose to share that information. I'll expect you at 14:00 tomorrow."

I opened my mouth to lodge another objection but his face gave me pause. Handsome yet intense, it was the kind of face that formed a natural barrier to the word 'no.'

"I am a prince of the two most formidable Houses in the realm," he said. "You would do well to stay on my good side."

The bastard had a good side? "I'll keep that in mind when consulting my schedule." Oops. It seemed my sarcasm was stronger than my will to live.

He dropped the paddle next to the board and walked away.

An invitation to the palace? I felt like Cinderella, except instead of a gown and glass slippers I'd be dressed in my finest armor with a cache of weapons tucked in all available crevices in case the prince got too frisky. I couldn't possibly go to the palace and yet it seemed I was unable to refuse. If the Demon of House Duncan demanded your presence, you showed up or risked him coming to find you. I definitely wouldn't want him angry when he tracked me down. I thought of how easily he snapped the selkie's neck and discarded her like a broken toy. Prince Callan was notorious throughout the realm for his power and cold indifference to life.

Retrieving my sheath, I shivered, but it wasn't because of the wind.

For the first time in many years, I was terrified.

5

I climbed the steps to my flat on the fifth floor that I affectionately referred to as the penthouse suite. The building itself was fairly rundown and maintenance never seemed to respond to the many requests, but it was in a prime location near the Euston train station and within walking distance to museums and the library, a place I liked to frequent. I was overdue for a visit. It wasn't exactly a home away from home—the staff recognized me, but our conversations didn't extend beyond pleasantries and the Dewey Decimal System.

I unlocked the door. It had been sticking lately, so I leaned my body weight against the edge to force it open. I spilled into the flat and nearly tripped over the red panda who was waiting patiently on the other side of the door. Red pandas were close to extinction and not native to the region. This one ended up coming home with me after a job involving a seller of endangered animals on the black market—for food.

"Hey, Big Red." The name was a misnomer since he was no bigger than a domestic cat, albeit with a slightly longer body. I scratched his reddish-brown fur. "I bet you're hungry." Like the others, Big Red was always hungry.

Jemima clucked as she made her way across the living room floor to greet me. The Bantam hen's diaper was droopy and I felt a stab of guilt. One of the reasons I resisted keeping a menagerie of animals was because...Well, the most important reason was because they violated the terms of my lease. I was allowed one pet and one pet only. The second most important reason was because I never knew how long I would be gone and I worried about leaving them too long. It couldn't be helped though. Jobs took however long they took and I didn't have the luxury of turning down work.

That particular thought stuck with me. Yes, I'd broken my own rule and turned down the prince's offer but that was different. Working for vampires—for House Lewis, no less—was too risky. My life wasn't worth the payout.

"I'll change that diaper in a few minutes, Jemima. Let me sort out the food first."

I sauntered into the kitchen where the rest of the crew awaited me. Their bellies were empty like clockwork. Hera, the calico cat, lorded over the rest of the animals even though she was the smallest. Her fierce attitude gave the illusion that she was much bigger. Her tri-color coat was the envy of the other animals. She was gorgeous and she knew it. She'd appeared outside the building a few years back during a brutal cold snap. I took pity on her and brought her inside. She never left.

The noise must've stirred Sandy from his slumber because the fennec fox appeared in the doorway, blinking and slightly disoriented. He tended to avoid the other animals, which was no small feat in a flat of this size. He acted disinterested in them, but I guaranteed if someone tried to mess with his flat mates, Sandy would be the first line of defense. When I met him, he was trying to take down a mischief of rats in Notting Hill. They'd backed him into a corner and he was not going down without a fight. I could've walked on by and let nature take its course, but his scrappy attitude compelled me to intervene. I thought he might turn on me the moment I finished clearing the path of rats. Instead he flicked those big ears and followed me home. I had no idea where he came from because he certainly wasn't native to England, but Sandy was one of us now and he seemed content with that.

"It's been quite a day," I announced. "I'll tell you about it as soon as we're settled."

In the living room, Herman bleated for my attention. Dissatisfied with the speed of my response, the black and white pygmy goat trotted over and pushed his horns against my side. I scratched behind his ear.

"Hello to you, too."

I set to work filling bowls with food and water before a mutiny occurred.

"You'll never guess what happened to me today," I rambled. "I fought a selkie and a vampire." I paused for dramatic effect. "Guess what else? This was no ordinary vampire. He's the Demon of House Duncan. He's so terrible that his own father sent him to live as a member of House Lewis." Not that King Casek was a lovable lamb. The ruler of House Lewis was fearsome in his own right and the only reason Callan was sent to live here was to pay penance for past aggressions. The offering of the only son and heir was a show of good faith that the Highland king would behave.

I fell silent and let everyone enjoy the contents of their respective bowls in peace and quiet. No one wanted my voice as the soundtrack that accompanied their meal.

I took the opportunity to pour myself a glass of filtered water and drank greedily. What must it have been like for a young Callan to be sent away to live with the enemy of his family? House Lewis and House Duncan were longtime rivals for control of England. It had to hurt.

I opened a tin of black beans and rinsed them before dumping half the contents into a flour tortilla. Meat wasn't exactly in abundance these days, but I was fairly certain I'd be a vegetarian regardless. My connection to animals was too strong to view any of them as food. Besides, legumes were easier and cheaper to source. I was always happy when a client offered to pay with protein. It saved me the trouble of shopping.

I only realized how hungry I truly was when I bit into the tortilla. Sagging against the counter, I took another enormous bite, still thinking about Prince Callan. At least he had two homes that wanted him. My home was the street for longer than I cared to remember. Some of those years were a blur. If I tried to bring the memories into clarity… There was little reason to remember any of it. I survived and that was all that mattered.

I ambled into the living room and opened the window that led to a makeshift balcony to check for Barnaby. One of the reasons this flat suited my needs was because of its 'outdoor space.' There was also a metal ladder that connected from the balcony to the rooftop which was convenient for some of the animals as well as for me.

I removed the hen's diaper and let her outside for fresh air. If she didn't feel the need to poop every twenty minutes, the diaper wouldn't be necessary, but I had no interest in searching for all the poop pellets after a long day of chasing monsters.

I dropped onto the sofa, physically and mentally

drained. It took a lot of effort to contain my magic. Using small bits of magic provided temporary relief, but I could never completely relax and I paid a price for the constant exertion.

Big Red jumped beside me and curled into a ball, his head resting on my thigh. I patted his head as I considered the prince's offer. It seemed too good to pass up and my inner child longed to see the inside of the royal palace. My mother once mentioned a visit there at the request of the royal tutor to demonstrate elemental magic to the children of staff. She'd spoken of the palace itself with reverence and a dreamy look in her eye, which was one of the reasons I remembered her account with such vividness. Rarely was my mother wistful. Her life had been hard up until her final moments and she'd hoped to spare me the challenges she faced. I didn't have the heart to tell her that her efforts were in vain. The mere fact of my existence meant my life would be an uphill battle.

I couldn't have the same dewy-eyed approach to the palace. My mother was a pureblood witch. She hadn't run the same risk by stepping foot inside a residence overrun with the most powerful vampires in the realm.

"Think of the money though," I said to no one in particular. It would be enough to tide me over for months. In Britannia City, that was the difference between survival and a visit to an early grave. I was healthy and strong, but it only took one bad stroke of luck to turn fortune's tide. One wound that took too long to heal. One encounter with the wrong people.

A knock on the door forced me to my feet. So rude. Didn't they know I'd had a long day? All I wanted now was a shower and sleep.

I opened the door and greeted Mona Keyes, my landlord. She didn't own the building though. She only managed it for a man called Elliot whom I'd never met. She was a stout woman with medium-brown hair the same shade as her eyes. Her skin was maybe half a shade lighter with gold undertones. Large freckles dotted her face and arms. When I first met her, I must've stared at her freckles for what seemed like an eternity. My mother once told me freckles were caused by the sun and yet somehow people managed to pass down the trait to their descendants. You didn't see them often, so when you did, you stared.

Or at least I did.

"How are you, Mona?"

She knocked on the wooden frame. "The door's sticking. I'll ask Bruno to fix it."

"Thanks, I was going to mention it. Want tea?"

"No, thank you. I'm here to give you notice we're getting new windows installed next week."

My eyebrows crept up. "The whole building?"

Nodding, she pushed her glasses to the bridge of her nose. At least they were connected to a chain around her neck. Judging from the number of times they slid, I guessed there were plenty of moments she missed and they dropped off her nose completely.

"They're past their best and some of the lower-floor windows have started to crack. Elliot wants all of them replaced at the same time."

"I smell a rent increase in my future."

She offered a weak smile. "Wouldn't surprise me."

"Will you be with them?" My flat was warded, but I'd carved an exception in the spell for Mona. She was the landlord. If there was an emergency, I needed her to be able to enter if I wasn't here. Of course, that presented a risk because multiple animals violated the lease, but I'd weighed the pros and cons and made what I felt was an informed decision.

"I'll let them in if you're not here, but I have no interest in hanging about while they work." She rolled her eyes. "You know how men are. It'll be all bawdy chatter. Half the time I swear it's to make me uncomfortable."

I mulled over the situation. I'd have to send the animals to the temporary realm I used in case of emergency, but they hated it there. The last time I sent them, Big Red expressed his displeasure upon his return by having explosive diarrhea all over the flat.

"You know, there's actually nothing wrong with my windows, so maybe you could skip mine. It's only the door I'd like fixed at the moment."

Mona pressed her lips together to form a thin line. "I'm not sure that will matter. Once Elliot gets a bee in his bonnet…" She shrugged. "You know how men are."

"I would appreciate it if you could let him know my windows are perfect as they are."

"I can tell you right now what the answer will be. He won't want to deal with yours later."

I begrudgingly accepted defeat. If I put up too much of a fight, they'd wonder why. I didn't need anyone suspicious of me.

One of the animals brushed against the back of my leg and I jerked the door so that there was only an inch gap. "If you'll excuse me, I'm desperate for a shower."

Mona sniffed the air. "Yes, I thought I smelled fish. You should really open the windows when you cook it."

"Good suggestion. I'll definitely do that next time." I started to close the door, but Mona wedged the toe of her shoe in the doorway to stop it.

"There's one more matter to discuss."

Uh oh. "What is it?"

"The rubbish collection schedule has changed to Mondays. If you put yours out too early, you'll be asked to bring it in. We don't need to attract pests. There are more than enough of those already."

"Noted. Thank you."

I closed the door and pressed my forehead against the doorjamb. I really needed to add an early warning system to my ward. I'd never forgive myself if I came home to find the animals gone. I knew exactly what would happen to them too. There'd be no rehoming. They'd end up on someone's dinner plate. Even Hera. These were desperate times for many people and they weren't above eating whatever meat they could get their hands on.

This seemed like a sign from the universe to accept the prince's offer. If I needed to change flats unexpectedly, I'd need the money to pay the security deposit plus first and last month's rent. It was money I didn't have.

I locked the door and turned to face the animals. "I can't take any chances. I'll have to send you to your holiday home until these windows are installed."

In the meantime, I'd do the job for House Lewis and collect the generous fee. If I needed the money to move, I'd have it. If not, it would be a nice nest egg.

I ignored the noises of disapproval and headed to the bathroom for a hot shower. I did some of my best thinking in there and right now I needed to strategize. Tomorrow I would enter the belly of the beast and I had to force myself to think through every possible scenario to quell my nerves. I needed to *feel* prepared for every outcome, however unrealistic.

I took extra time in the shower, letting the warm water slide down my skin. I scrubbed every inch of my body and washed my hair twice. Pure decadence. If today was my last full day on earth, I figured I might as well take a moment to enjoy the little things.

After I dressed, I patted every head in the flat, tossed a handful of seeds outside for Barnaby, and said a silent prayer before falling into bed. My words would fall on deaf ears, I knew, but I pretended they mattered all the same.

Sometimes the only way to make it through this life was to pretend I was living a very different one.

6

A silver statue of Britannia greeted me as I skirted the monument on my way to the palace. Not too fast or too slow. No movement that would raise the suspicions of security. The vampire queen rose from the earth like a silver butterfly from her concrete cocoon. Five figures surrounded the base of the statue, each one representing a House she defeated to become the leading royal family in the region—Peyton in the Southwest, Duncan in Scotland, Osmond across the Strait of Dover, Kane in Wales, and Troy in Ireland. Modesty, thy name is not Britannia.

House Lewis spared no expense to maintain the grandeur of the palace. Since the Great Eruption, most buildings in the city had fallen into disrepair or were left in ruins because the owners couldn't afford the costly repairs or upkeep. Not this one. The French neoclassical style of the facade was lovingly preserved, along with the balcony where the royal family addressed their adoring crowds. Or so I'd been told. Any crowd that involved vampires didn't include me.

I steadied my breathing and slowed my heart rate.

Walking into a building full of vampires was risky enough. Walking into the palace of the most powerful vampire House in the realm was borderline insane, not that I had much choice. His Highland Highness made it pretty darn clear that I was the Chosen One for this particular task and no other expendable minion would do.

A row of guards stood sentry in front of the gates. Every vampire assigned to royal security was a lethal killer given carte blanche to act on a perceived threat. If I so much as raised a hand too quickly, I'd lose it. This was my last chance to back away slowly. I allowed one final glance at my skin—no sign of silver. Quelling my nerves, I approached the imposing gates of the palace.

The guards didn't react to my presence. They seemed to know my arrival was expected. Instead of the usual tingling sensation I felt in the presence of vampires, my skin was on fire. Danger, my body shrieked. Ahead of me the palace loomed, splendid yet foreboding.

The gates opened and I strode toward the entrance with purpose, taking comfort in the weapons strapped to my back and my thigh. It was a false sense of security, of course. No matter how many weapons I carried inside, I would still be one person against the entire royal guard.

A gap appeared as the doors opened to welcome me. I was mildly surprised by their willingness to admit me without stripping me of my weapons, but I chalked that up to hubris. House Lewis was the royal vampire family for a reason. Their bloody past was prominent in recent history books. At the start of the Eternal Night, Britannia Lewis led the family to power and greatness, supplanting the humans who were no longer fit to rule, and was honored with a city and palace that now bore her name.

A butler greeted me at the door wearing a dark red tail-coat and a crisp white shirt underneath. Another vampire. Most employees of the royal residences were vampires because they didn't trust outsiders nor did they trust another species to do a job as well.

The butler bowed. "Good afternoon, miss."

"London Hayes. Knights of Boudica."

He bowed again. "May I unburden you?"

He was asking to relieve me of my weapons. Nope. Not a chance.

"I'm good, thanks."

"In that case, if you'll please follow me."

"Gladly."

Although I'd seen old photographs of the palace interior, they looked nothing like the rooms before me now. Once House Lewis took control of the palace, they did more than change the name. Queen Britannia modified the entire interior space so that it would be unrecognizable to visitors and impenetrable by her enemies. My mother told me that Buckingham Palace had been open to the public when it was occupied by human residents. Britannia didn't want her enemies to be able to use the widely available information in order to identify weaknesses or entry points. She was a paranoid queen, and for good reason. Ever since the vampires emerged from the shadows, the Houses were under constant threat, not only from other species but from each other. No vampire House seemed content to be second best. They lost a battle or a war, and then they licked their wounds and bided their time until they felt revitalized enough to try, try again.

The butler guided me to a cavernous room with gleaming marble floors and the highest ceilings I'd ever seen. Crystal seemed to sparkle everywhere I looked. Chandeliers. Glassware. There was even a crystal elephant on display atop a marble column. Crystal seemed an odd choice for a species endangered by sunlight. A statue of Britannia took pride of place under a curved archway at the far end of the room and I walked closer to inspect it. Her form was perfect, although I could've done without the splashes of red around her mouth and dripping between her breasts.

My skin began to crawl. I had company.

I blinked and the Horror of the Highlands stood beside me. He wore a dark cloak over his clothes. His dark blond hair was slightly damp and curled at the ends as though he'd emerged from the bathtub mere moments ago. I tried not to picture him emerging from a bathtub or a shower or anything else that invoked his naked body.

"Impressive, isn't she?" Words poured from his sensuous mouth, smooth like whisky. "Welcome to House Lewis, Miss Hayes."

I quickly regained my composure. Show no weakness or he'd show no mercy. "I'm surprised you'd pay her the compliment."

It was Queen Britannia who'd successfully defended the city against an attack by House Duncan. She died during the infamous Battle of Britannia, but not before claiming victory for House Lewis and exhausting the Highland forces. It was also thanks to her that a young prince was delivered to the palace doorstep as a hostage to be raised by House Lewis. According to scholars, it had been a sticking point in the negotiations and King Casek had insisted the provision be upheld in honor of his late wife.

The prince turned his gaze to the statue. "I have come to admire her achievements without bitterness."

I decided to shift gears, not wanting to stir unpleasant

memories any further. "Do you always walk around your house invisible?"

"Only when I'm not in the mood to be seen." He paused and looked at me expectantly. "Most women in my presence attempt a curtsy at the very least." His lips curved into a smile. "More than a few like to flash a bit of cleavage while they're down there as well."

I offered an exaggerated bow instead. Alas, there'd be no cleavage on display even if I were so inclined—which I most definitely wasn't. The design of my uniform was similar to a scuba suit. It was fairly asexual as far as uniforms went, which suited me just fine.

"Good enough." He motioned to a highbacked chair swathed in crushed red velvet. Red was the accent color of choice throughout the palace. The drapery. The upholstery. Even the statue of the former queen. Every vampire House claimed red as their signature color, but I was willing to bet only House Lewis managed to do it with such panache.

I perched on the edge of the chair, prompting a smile from His Royal Rapscallion.

"You might be more comfortable if you remove the sheath."

"I'm fine, thank you." I made a show of settling against the chair, treating the bulk of weapons on my back like a soft pillow.

Another vampire entered the room to offer us refreshments.

"No thank you," I said.

"It isn't the underworld," the prince said. "You may eat from our stock and still be free to leave afterward."

"Thank you. The answer is still no." My body remained on high alert and the sooner I could escape the palace, the better.

The prince turned to address the staff member. "In that case, nothing for me for now. Thank you."

How gallant.

He removed his cloak and set it across the back of the adjacent chair, revealing form-fitting trousers that left little to the imagination.

"What do you think?" he asked. "Big enough for you?"

My mouth turned to cotton. "I beg your pardon?"

The prince smiled. "The palace."

Heat warmed my cheeks. "It's quite impressive."

His smile broadened as he sat on the chair adjacent to mine. Only a small round table separated us.

"It's been almost exactly like this since I moved here. The king doesn't share the same interest in interior design as his former queen."

"And what about Queen Imogen?"

King Casek remarried within two years of Britannia's death, sparking an outcry from those vampires fiercely loyal to the queen. The king wisely chose Imogen, a daughter of House Osmond. An alliance with vampires from across the English Channel made sense from a strategic point. Britannia had been the more intimidating one in their partnership. Without her, House Lewis risked having to defend their territory yet again once another House grew strong enough to attempt an overthrow.

The prince's gaze traveled around the room. "I see a few acquisitions, but Mother's too practical to splash out on knickknacks she doesn't need."

"In other words, we won't find statues in Her Highness's likeness strewn across the city."

His eyebrows inched up at the slight but he said nothing. I needed to show better sense. I wasn't among friends. The opposite, really. Dead or not, a barbed comment about

Queen Britannia in her own palace was foolish even for me.

"How can I help you, Your Highness?" I struggled not to choke on the reverential title. Did I have a problem with authority? Why, yes. Yes, I did. Was that problem exacerbated when the authority figure was a vampire? Yes, it was.

"It's a delicate matter, one that requires discretion."

"Which is one of the reasons we're hiring from outside our usual pool of knights," a voice interjected.

My magic flared in response and I suppressed the urge to protect myself. I glanced over to see another vampire stride into the room with an air of importance. He and Prince Callan were night and day personified. Where Callan was fair and blond, this vampire was dark-haired with olive skin and deep brown eyes. Like Callan, however, he radiated danger.

"Miss Hayes, may I introduce Prince Maeron?"

Oh, crap. No wonder my magical system was flooding.

I sprang to my feet and offered a half-hearted bow, taking a quick moment to check my bare skin for signs of a silver glow.

Still good.

Maeron's dark eyes twinkled with amusement. "I suppose my brother has brought you up to speed on the situation."

"I was just getting to it," Callan said. He seemed miffed by the interruption.

Maeron stood beside his brother's chair and placed a casual arm across its back. "Must you leave cloaks hanging from every available surface." He tugged the cloak from the chair and folded it over his arm.

I bit back a smile. Sibling squabbles over untidiness. Not the conversation I expected in the palace. I began to feel more at ease, although I'd have a death wish if I let down my guard completely.

"You don't look like a knight," Maeron said.

I raised my chin to meet his curious gaze. "And what should a knight look like in your world?"

"For starters, you don't have the right equipment."

"Pray tell, when was the last time any of your knights completed a quest using his penis?" I asked.

Callan choked back laughter.

Maeron smiled, showing a set of razor-sharp fangs.

Nice try, honey. I've seen bigger.

"And now I understand your choice, brother," Maeron said. "Adwin should be here any moment. I passed him coming up from the cellars."

On cue, a third vampire entered the room pushing a two-tiered cart in front of him. The side of the cart was etched in silver and both tiers were crammed with long-necked bottles. The cart alone was fancier than anything in my flat.

"Adwin is our House winemaker," Callan said. "He's the best in the realm."

"That says quite a lot about you, Adwin." Wine was a luxury the average person couldn't afford. Vineyards failed to thrive without magical intervention, which created scarcity. Naturally the Houses had no shortage of magic helpers. As a result, they controlled production as well as prices.

Adwin smiled and I noticed that he kept his teeth square. Interesting. "They flatter me because they know I hold the key to the cellars," he said.

There seemed to be more pleasantries involved in this meeting than I anticipated. Was I here as a knight or a guest of honor?

"What do you have for us today, old chap?" Maeron asked. "Please don't tell me it's another Bordeaux. I've had quite enough of anything French."

Callan chuckled.

I sensed a story there, although I had no idea what it was. I didn't follow royal gossip. Information about vampires was only of interest when it helped me avoid them.

Adwin gestured to the cart. "I have a selection as requested, Your Highness, as well as your preferred vintage."

"Very good, Adwin," Callan said with a nod of approval.

Maeron rolled his eyes. "Such a diva."

His brother snorted. "Says the one who wants to avoid all things French because of one rejection."

Nostrils flaring, Maeron whirled around to face his brother. "I was *not* rejected. It was a simple misunderstanding. How was I to know she was already engaged to that German twat?"

Adwin cleared his throat. "Shall I pour?"

Maeron waved a hand. "Mine first. The Basque, please."

The winemaker uncorked a bottle and the stench nearly gagged me. This wasn't wine.

Maeron's vintage of choice was blood.

Adwin seemed to pick up on my apprehension because he quickly said, "A pinot noir for you, Miss Hayes? Or perhaps a claret?"

I opted for a glass of pinot noir if only to distract myself from the smell of blood. I tasted the wine and let the rich blend of flavors soak my tongue. I could count on one hand the number of times I'd enjoyed a glass of wine. The last time was when I was admitted as a Knight of Boudica. Kami and I had splurged on a bottle and split it between the two of us. The wine had been expensive but not particularly good. This bottle, on the other hand, was incredible.

"Can you believe there was a time when wine was so plentiful people spat mouthfuls into a vat?" Maeron asked.

"Abundance only leads to waste, Your Highness," Adwin agreed.

Callan poured his own glass of wine. "I think we ought to tell our guest why she's here."

Please do.

"Our dear sister has gone missing," Maeron said.

Callan shot him a disgruntled look. "A bit of finesse might have been nice."

I swallowed hard, forcing down the mouthful of wine. "I'm sorry. Did you say the princess is missing?"

"That's why you're here," Maeron said.

I cast an aggrieved look at Callan. "This is the job? Find a missing princess?"

"What's the issue? Don't think you're capable?" Callan let the question hang between us.

"Davina was following a lead on a confidential matter," Maeron interrupted. "And she seems to have gone walkabout in the process."

Taking another sip of wine, I inhaled its intense aroma of black cherry and cinnamon. If nothing else, this glass of wine was worth the price of admission to the palace. It also helped relieve the tension in my body.

"If you expect me to track her, it would help to know what lead she was following."

Maeron grunted. "I don't think that's necessary."

"Ah, excellent. Our knight is here." A statuesque woman entered the room wearing a floor-length dress that hugged small breasts and narrow hips. The fabric was a deep emerald green that matched Callan's eyes—not that I'd taken special notice of them.

The vampire queen halted at the sight of me, frowning. "Who is this?"

I didn't need to ask who she was. Her high cheek bones and regal air gave her away.

I jumped to my feet and bowed. "London Hayes at your service, Your Majesty."

She turned to the wine cart. "Excellent. I've been parched for the past hour." She examined the selection. "The Basque, please, Adwin."

"Like mother, like son," Adwin said.

"Stepson," Maeron corrected him.

I noticed the queen stiffen in response. Queen Imogen replaced Britannia in the king's bed as well as on the throne. That couldn't have been an easy pill to swallow for a young boy with vivid memories of his famous and powerful mother.

Adwin poured from the bottle and I averted my gaze rather than watch the blood slide into the long-stemmed glass. The stench alone was enough to turn my stomach.

The queen nodded to me. "You may sit."

My head told me to sit, but my body urged me to flee. I was now in a room with three members of House Lewis, one of the most feared vampire families in the world. What was I thinking? This was suicide. Any moment now, I'd start to glow silver. If that happened, they'd kill me right here, right now, and no one would ever know what became of me.

"Will Father be joining our meeting?" Maeron asked.

"He's occupied with other matters at present," the queen said.

What matter could be more important than the disappearance of his daughter?

Callan offered his chair but the queen politely declined. He resumed a standing position so that no one was seated.

"So what does our fair knight think about the stone?" the queen asked.

So much for confidential matters.

I seized the moment. "They were just getting to that," I said.

"Very good. Probably best if I explain." The queen sipped from her glass. "Davina was acquiring an item of interest for our House. That's when she disappeared. We'd like you to find the stone."

I blinked in confusion. "You want me to focus on finding the stone rather than your daughter?" I could understand her disinterest if Princess Davina had been born to Britannia, but she was the queen's own natural-born daughter.

Imogen drank before answering. "I have every confidence Davina is fine. She's simply following in her older brother's difficult footsteps."

Maeron glowered at her. "An unnecessary jab, Mother."

"Davina is young and impulsive," the queen continued. "She's heard tales of Maeron's exploits and hopes to copy them. I'm certain it's nothing more than that. Oats must be sown, after all."

Interesting that the princes seemed more concerned about Davina than her own mother. Usually it would be the other way around.

"What can you tell me about the stone?" I asked.

The queen nodded crisply. "Indeed. Last week we dined with an antiquities dealer. He mentioned a stone and said he'd never seen anything like it. He's a fascinating man, well-versed in history, which is why he's a frequent guest here."

"It helps that he always brings a trinket for you," Maeron commented drily.

Her lips curved into a satisfied smile. "It certainly doesn't hurt."

So the queen disliked knickknacks for display but was a fan of trinkets. Got it.

"I asked him for a description and it sounded like the perfect artifact for my collection," she continued.

"What about it appealed to you?" I asked.

The queen faltered. "Its simplicity. The owner, Maria, had apparently discovered the stone at an excavation site. It sounded quite primitive."

"It was found in the city?" I asked.

The queen nodded. "Yes. The former site of St. Paul's Cathedral. Do you know it?"

"Yes. Why would a stone's simplicity appeal to you?"

The queen's fingers fidgeted along the stem of her glass. "That's my taste, I suppose."

One look at the sparkling 'trinket' clasped around her neck told a different story.

An awkward silence ensued. They were hiding something. I was sure of it. Their story was far too flimsy. They were probably so accustomed to doing as they pleased, they'd lost the ability to weave a credible tale.

"How did the princess end up involved?" I probed.

"I instructed the dealer to acquire the stone for us at any price. The owner agreed to sell and Davina was dispatched to make the transaction."

"She begged to be involved," Maeron added. "I told her she was better off planning another gala. That's what other seventeen-year-old princesses do. They don't gallivant around the realm like some kind of common…"

"Knight?" I offered.

At least Maeron had the decency to appear embarrassed.

Callan wore a wry smile. "And how did our fair sister respond to that?"

"About as well as you can imagine," Maeron replied.

Callan shifted his focus to me. "When she failed to return, I went in search of her. I found the owner of the stone encased in metal, like a corpse in a molten coffin." He snapped his fingers to someone in the corridor and a vampire entered holding a large envelope. The vampire opened the envelope and emptied the contents into the prince's hands. "I took photographs."

He moved to stand beside me and I studied the background. "The owner lived in quite an opulent place."

"Oh, no. That's a room in the palace," Callan said.

My brow creased. "I thought you found the owner elsewhere."

"I did, but I wasn't about to leave behind the only bit of evidence."

I nearly choked. "You *carried* this? By yourself?" Solid metal like this had to weigh…I didn't want to contemplate it.

He grinned. "Have I finally managed to impress you?"

There was no way I could've carried the metal cocoon. No doubt the reason he brought me the photos.

"We can't identify the type of metal," Maeron said. "It's unlike anything we've ever seen."

"I have a sample if you'd like to take it with you for further examination," Callan offered.

"I would."

Now I understood why they needed a knight and why they needed one from a different banner than their usual ones. If word got out that a princess of House Lewis was missing, it would make the royal family appear weak. They wanted this kept quiet. The assignment was more complicated than I anticipated.

I looked at the queen. "And there's been no ransom note, Your Majesty?"

The queen shook her head. "No communication of any kind. Not even to gloat." She shot a pointed look at Callan. "Which is one of the reasons I believe she's absolutely fine and enjoying the air of mystery."

"The owner of the stone *died*," Callan stressed. "The stone and Davina are now missing. What about those circumstances suggests that Davina is absolutely fine?"

I didn't know much about the princess, but I was inclined to agree.

"I'll need a description of the stone." Searching for a stone in the rubble of Britannia City was akin to searching for a drop of water in the ocean.

"I'll have it for you before you leave," the queen said.

"That's assuming you accept the job," Callan added.

Maeron snorted. "Who wouldn't accept a job from House Lewis? She'd have to be mad."

"How about it, Miss Hayes? Are you mad?" The Highland Reckoning raised his eyebrows at me. A challenge.

I'd been willing to entertain the offer because of their stature and the payment involved, but now they'd given me another compelling reason. I couldn't take the thought of a young woman in peril, even if she was a vampire. Davina was only seventeen. Vampire or not, I knew exactly how it felt to be a vulnerable young woman alone in the city.

I grew up in the long shadow of fear, but eventually I had to learn to stop being afraid. That didn't mean I stopped hiding. To show my true self was suicide. It just meant to stop letting fear control me the way it had controlled my mother. Once I was born, her entire life centered around my safety. Every choice she made. She quit her job and moved flats. She used her magic to hide our scents. She didn't allow herself any friendships and certainly not any romantic relationships.

And because she was alone, after she died, I was too.

I clenched my fingers so no one noticed my hand trembling. "I'll start immediately," I said.

The queen polished off her drink and handed the stained glass to Adwin. "Splendid."

7

I left the palace, made one quick stop, and continued straight to the Circus. Now that I'd officially accepted the job, I needed a plan. There was very little to go on. A hunk of metal no one could identify. A nondescript stone from an excavation site. A missing princess.

I had my work cut out for me.

"Back so soon?" Minka asked as I entered the Pavilion. "Didn't we see you yesterday?"

"What can I say? I missed you. Plus I promised to replenish Stevie's snacks." I held up a bag.

"I was wondering what happened to my emergency stash." Stevie Torrin slid open her desk drawer.

"You changed your hair. Looks good." The ends of her dark hair had been dyed silver to match the undertones of her brown skin.

"I told her to go for magenta," Kami said.

Stevie shook her head. "Too close to red."

Sniffing the air between us, Minka frowned. "You smell wrong."

I edged away from her. "Gee, thanks. And your disposition is delightful as always."

Minka wasn't put off by my snark. "Where were you?"

I shook the bag. "At the shop."

Her eyes narrowed. "No, before that."

Damn Minka and her sense of smell. You'd think she was a shifter with that nose, but you'd be wrong.

"I had a meeting."

Minka scrunched her nose. "In a graveyard? You reek of death and violence."

I glanced down at my clothes. Although it wasn't unusual for me to show up covered in blood and guts, today wasn't one of those days.

"She couldn't have had a meeting in a graveyard," Stevie interrupted. "She wouldn't have made it back here so quickly."

"Could've been a pre-Eternal Night graveyard," Minka countered.

I dumped the contents of the bag into the gaping drawer.

"Thanks," Stevie said.

I shut the drawer with my foot. "No problem."

Minka shook her head. "It's not a graveyard."

I didn't enjoy my time under the microscope and intended to beat a hasty treat before the questions increased. I leaned down to sign the report waiting on my desk and handed it to Minka.

"I only came in to fill out paperwork," I lied. "See you tomorrow."

I'd have to figure out my plan in the comfort of my flat where the only questions asked were 'where's my dinner?' and 'can you open the window so I can pee?'

I'd steer clear of the Circus until the job was over if I

could help it. If the other knights knew I was working for House Lewis, there'd be hell to pay.

I hefted my bag over my shoulder and started for the exit.

Kami rolled her chair in front of me to block my exit. "And where do you think you're going?"

"Home to scrub the stench of death and violence off me, apparently."

Her jaw clicked. "I don't think so. You're coming out with us. We want all the details of your day." She leveled me with a look. "And I do mean all."

I ran my tongue over my teeth. I should've known better than to think I could fool anyone here. The Knights of Boudica were incredible at what they did, not only because they were fierce fighters, but because they paid attention to details. They didn't walk into a room and immediately try to dominate the space. They took a moment to assess the players, get a handle on their strengths and weaknesses, maybe even what they had for breakfast if the information was useful. They fought smarter. I appreciated their skills in the field. Not so much when they used them against me.

"Who's up for a drink?" Kami called across the room.

Hands went up.

Nope. I wasn't getting out of this one. I squared my shoulders. Fine. I'd be a joiner. Depending on how this case progressed, I might need to call on the other knights for help, although I'd try my best to avoid it. It was better to handle things on my own whenever possible. I didn't want to endanger my friends. Our job was dangerous enough without my secret making it worse. A typical witch might seek gainful employment from an influential vampire and be rewarded with a comfortable lifestyle that included healthcare and protection from other vampires. For knights, violence was a way of life and when we lost, we ended up either burned on a pyre or buried outside the city, depending on the circumstances.

When I became a knight, I signed a document that told the banner my burial wishes. Standard stuff so there's no debate. Usually there isn't time for a discussion with the family, if there is one. Decisions have to be made and made quickly. If you want to be buried, there are only a few trains per week that carry the dead outside the city and arrangements have to be made. Buried or burned means your body won't end up in the hands of vampires. Although there's an official system in place via tribute centers, some of the more predatory vampires aren't above taking advantage of an unfortunate situation.

"Let's go now before London gets called away on an emergency," Kami said.

I could've strangled her. She knew me well enough to know I was hiding something and she wasn't going to let me walk away without extracting the information.

"If anybody owes me a report, please do it before leaving," Minka announced. For a knight, she was oddly obsessed with paperwork. Kami once said the world dodged a bullet when Minka wasn't born a vampire.

We ignored Minka and filed out of the Pavilion. No one bothered to say where we were headed. We all knew. There was only one pub in the neighborhood we agreed on and that was The Crown. It was an old pub noteworthy for keeping its original stained-glass windows intact. The walls, once a dark brown, were painted an off white, as many interiors were, to better reflect the limited light available. Strings of lights crisscrossed the ceiling, giving the walls a slightly yellow sheen. The tables were small except for one oval table toward the back that the owner kept reserved for larger parties and us. If people were seated there when we arrived, Simon would move them to another table without a second thought. He took good care of his regulars.

Behind the bar Simon brightened upon seeing us enter. He liked us because we tipped well and we weren't prone to property damage like some of his other clientele. Simon was a werewolf and shapeshifters preferred to frequent pubs owned by other shapeshifters, which was good news for him except when a brawl broke out. When it came to shapeshifters, that happened more often than not. The other upside was that vampires generally considered a shapeshifter-owned pub to be beneath them, so we knew it was a safe haven from the establishment. Then again, I'd thought the same about the Hole until Prince Callan showed up.

I pushed aside thoughts of the royal vampire and his intense green eyes. Not interested. Not even a little bit.

The Crown was fairly empty at this hour. Too late for the lunch crowd and too early for the evening crowd. I called it the Goldilocks hour because it was just right for me.

I tried to plant my butt in a middle seat, but Kami grabbed my shoulder and steered me to the end of the oval. The hot seat. Terrific.

Kami raised a finger at Simon. "One round, please." She sat beside me and clasped her hands on the table. "Now that we're all listening without distractions, why don't you tell us about your meeting today, London?"

I pictured myself pinning her to the wall and head-butting her, but that was no way to treat your best friend—was it?

Then again, this was no way for my best friend to treat me. She knew I was dodging questions, which only increased her desire to extract the information from me. She should trust that I had a good reason for keeping quiet.

Simon carried over two pitchers of ale and set them on the table, quickly followed by a basket of rolls.

Stevie pulled a pitcher closer to her. "What's everyone else having?"

"Yes, yes," Simon said. "Point taken. I'll fetch the glasses."

"Who's hungry?" Stevie asked.

Kami pulled a face. "What kind of question is that?"

Simon returned with a stack of glassware and set one in front of each of us. "I've got two types of pie today. Kidney and homity."

"One of each for the table, please," Stevie said.

Simon gave a curt nod and hustled away. He knew better than to leave us hungry for long. We wouldn't bust up the pub, but we were champions at complaining.

"Spill," Kami demanded. "And I'm not talking about your ale."

I tipped back my head and groaned. "Fine, but you have to promise not to give me a hard time."

"Can't promise when we don't know what you're about to say."

At least she was honest.

Kami poured the golden liquid into my glass. "Drink first. Then talk."

I obeyed. "I took a job for a vampire family."

Everyone at the table gasped. Actually, I was pretty sure Simon gasped too. He'd emerged from the kitchen with a stack of plates for the table.

Stevie's brow creased. "Why would you do that?"

"Mack sent it to me. He didn't realize. There was a middleman involved."

Minka tapped the outside of her glass. "Why would they hire one of us?"

I swallowed a mouthful of ale. "They want to keep the job quiet. Another banner would involve too much red tape and require details they don't want public."

Kami smacked her lips after polishing off her ale. "Don't want public? How important are these vampires?"

I grasped for an appropriate response. "They have a lot of employees and a lot of money. They don't want the information to be used against them."

There. That sounded reasonable.

Kami scrutinized me. "You're leaving out the most important part."

I cursed the day I ever met Kamikaze Marwin in a damp, rat-infested tunnel. "No, I'm not."

Kami laughed. "You're the worst liar."

"She's actually quite good," Stevie said. "I wouldn't suspect a thing if it weren't for you."

I shot Kami a pointed look.

"That's only because you're listening to her voice and not looking at her face," Kami objected.

Minka folded her arms and regarded me. "If you're involved in an assignment that could have repercussions for the rest of us, I think we're entitled to know. In fact, I insist."

She insisted? Now I was thoroughly annoyed.

I downed my drink and set the empty glass on the table. "I'm withholding that information for your own protection."

Simon returned with a cloth to wipe down the table.

"Don't you normally wait until we leave to do that?" Minka asked.

"I would, but then I won't be able to hear London's answer."

My stare must've been sufficiently hard because he scuttled back behind the bar.

"I've been hired by House Lewis," I whispered.

The table erupted with questions and possibly a few swear words.

"This makes no sense," Stevie said. "Why would they hire you?"

"I told you. They want to keep the job quiet, which is why I didn't want to tell you."

"Did they make you sign a confidentiality agreement?" Minka asked.

"No, but they made it clear they expect me to keep my involvement quiet." And the last thing I wanted to do was get on the wrong side of royal vampires.

"But we don't work for vampires," Stevie said.

"On principle, not on paper," I reminded her. It was an unwritten rule.

"Exactly," Stevie said. "So what happened to yours?"

I leveled her with a look. "Do you really see this as a choice?"

"London's right," Minka interjected. "If it this were a regular vampire, it would be easier. We can't risk the wrath of the royal family. We'd lose our license to practice magic."

"Or worse," Kami added. "What's the job?"

I sighed. I knew that would be the next question. "I can't say."

"Fair enough," Stevie said. "I think the less we know, the better."

"Gee, I'm so glad you agree with the way I intended to handle this from the outset until someone strong-armed me." I glared at Kami.

Kami gave her head a hard shake. "I don't like it."

"Of course you don't. She's working for the worst of the

worst," Stevie said. "House Lewis didn't seize power due to their cuddly natures."

Kami finished her beer and poured another one. "Did you meet all of them?"

"No, but I met enough." I couldn't say too much without revealing Princess Davina's situation.

Simon delivered two pies to the table and everyone pounced at once. I must've been hungrier than I realized because I didn't even like kidney pie, but I ate a slice without objection or an effort to trade.

"Did they force you to drink blood?" Minka asked.

Kami's nostrils flared in annoyance. "Why would they do that? She's not a vampire."

"Can you imagine meeting the Demon of House Duncan?" Minka shuddered. "I've seen him from a safe distance. I think he might be able to drain your blood with a single look."

"I heard he can lift an entire building," Stevie added.

I remembered the metal cocoon. "Anything's possible," I said, non-committal.

Stevie looked at me expectantly. "You met him?"

I pressed my fingers to my temples. This was exactly the scenario I hoped to avoid. "Like you said, the less you all know, the safer it is."

Kami poured herself another drink from the pitcher. "I still don't like it."

"I don't either, but what was the alternative? Say no to House Lewis? That would've gone down really well."

Kami pressed her lips together. I understood her concern better than anybody, but I was backed into a corner and the only way out was to comply.

"I'll do the job, collect payment, and sail off into the sunset."

At the mention of sunset, everyone fell silent. We knew what the expression meant, but the only sunsets we'd ever seen were in photographs or artwork and they were spectacular. The intensity of the colors. The way the whole sky was illuminated. It seemed incredible that there was once a world where a sun rose and set every single day. The people alive then must've taken them for granted. I couldn't imagine what it must've been like for that initial generation to wake up one day steeped in darkness. They must've expected the horror to eventually end.

They died still waiting.

"If you need any help, please don't hesitate to ask," Stevie said. "I know it's meant to be a low-key operation, but I'm not about to let one of us get abused by vampires."

"I have no intention of getting abused." I could take care of myself in that regard, although I had to be more careful than usual.

"You know London won't ask," Kami said. "We'll simply have to watch her for any sign of trouble."

"No need for any stalkers," I said. I already had one of those. Any more and it would turn into a parade.

We finished the pies and pitchers and I left the pub in a good mood, which was unexpected. I assumed the disclosure would leave me feeling annoyed and exposed, but I actually felt better.

As we turned a corner, I sensed someone watching me. I pivoted to see three sets of red eyes observing me from the shadows of a nearby alley.

"Trio?"

The dog trotted forward.

"What are you doing here?" I patted each head.

"I took her to another end of the city," Kami said. "She must've found her way back here." She dug into her pocket and produced a roll she'd taken from the pub for later. She tore it into three pieces and fed each one to a head.

"What are we going to do with you, huh?" I scratched behind her ear.

"Nothing," Minka said. "The answer is we're going to do nothing with her. She's big enough to swallow a pony. She can fend for herself."

I cupped her jowls. "You wouldn't eat a pony, would you? Who's such a good girl?"

"What if she stayed at the Pavilion?" Kami asked. "We could use an extra layer of security, especially now that we know what London's up to."

Minka looked at Trio and wrinkled her nose. "A guard dog?"

Kami rubbed the dog's head. "Why not? Trio's obviously taken to us and needs something to occupy her so she doesn't end up in trouble."

"I think she'll end up in trouble in the Pavilion," Stevie said. "If we leave her there unattended, I guarantee we'll come back in the morning to a complete mess."

Minka nodded, her resistance strengthening. "Stevie's right. And who's going to pay for the cleanup? What if she eats critical documents?"

"You wouldn't eat paper, would you?" I stroked her back. "Of course not. You have taste."

"Let's put it to a vote," Kami said.

Minka exhaled sharply. "We can't. Not everyone's here."

"All in favor?" Kami pressed, ignoring the objection.

Kami, Stevie and I raised our hands.

"Majority rules." Kami gave the dog a triumphant pat on the back.

"The question is who's going to take her back to the Pavilion now?" Minka asked.

We exchanged wary glances. The Circus was in the opposite direction from my flat. On the other hand, I was the one who brought Trio into our lives. It seemed only fair for me to escort her.

"I'll do it."

Trio seemed to understand the conversation and three tongues dropped to the sides of three mouths. She was either happy or plotting world domination. Maybe both.

"I'll go with you if you want," Kami said, in a way that suggested she'd rather not but she was too good a friend not to offer.

"No. It's my mess. I'll handle it." I made a clicking sound and Trio loped forward to follow me. "See you later."

The Pavilion was only a block and a half away. I'd settle the dog in and make it home in time for a bath before bed. If I ended up cutting it too close to bedtime, I'd shower instead, but I really wanted the bath tonight. I wanted to scrub all traces of vampire interaction from my body.

Treena was still on duty when we entered the building. She didn't seem thrilled to see the return of the three-headed dog.

"What happened? Did she bite someone?"

"Nope. We offered her a job in exchange for food and shelter."

Treena's eyebrows lifted. "Here?"

I scratched behind her closest ear. "She's your backup."

"Why do I need backup? I have an entire banner of knights and their armory behind me."

"Not when the building's closed. Trio's going to be here all the time."

"What about walks? Won't she need to do her business?"

"She's got the bladder of a camel." I had no idea if that

was true, but I really wanted that bath and the longer I argued with Treena, the less likely the bath would happen.

"Three mouths and one bladder? I find that hard to believe."

Damn Treena and her common sense.

"I think I need to run this past Minka."

I smiled. "She objected."

"I figured."

"She was also outvoted."

Treena popped a hand on her ample hip. "Let me guess. You, Kami, and Stevie said yes."

I wagged a finger at her. "If I didn't know any better, I'd say you were psychic."

I started forward but Treena held out an arm to block me. "I'm going to need the approval in writing from Minka. Sorry, London. It's in the rulebook. If I let you leave this monster here, I'm risking my job."

"There's a rule about hiring three-headed dogs as part of the security team?"

"Not specifically, but it would fall under the provision that addresses overnight guests."

I swore under my breath. Minka *knew* there was a rule. That was the reason she didn't fight harder.

I glanced at Trio. "I guess you're hanging out with me tonight." I had no idea how I would sneak the beast into my flat without anyone noticing, but I'd give it my best shot. *I* could turn invisible, but I couldn't turn my companions invisible.

"I don't have space for a permanent addition," I told Trio as we left the Circus and headed toward Euston. "I can squeeze you in for one night though. Just try not to intimidate the others. They pretend to be tough, but they're pretty fragile."

I managed to usher Trio into the building and upstairs without incident. One of the reasons I chose this flat was because it was quiet and the neighbors kept to themselves. I introduced Trio to the menagerie and laid out the ground rules. The animals knew what would happen if they picked a fight.

I turned on the bathtub tap and walked back to the kitchen to scrounge up food for my new guest, who was currently sprawled across the living room floor.

A knock on the door startled me. *Whoever you are, now is not a good time.*

I hurried to the bathroom to stop the water running. The tub was half full. I poured a few bubbles in and swirled them around.

The knocking continued. My visitor was persistent, I'd give him that.

I ran to the door and opened it about an inch. Not him. Her.

"Hey, Mona."

"So sorry to disturb you, but the tenant in 3B swears he saw you leading a three-headed monster up the steps to your flat."

I barked a laugh. "Three heads? How drunk was he?"

The landlord offered a timid smile. "I know it sounds absurd, but stranger things have been seen in the city and it wouldn't be the first time someone claimed you brought an illegal animal into the building."

Yeah. My reputation was questionable at best. Fortunately no one could ever prove anything so I managed to break dozens of rules without consequences. I realized that was nothing to be proud of, but there were times when I was willing to put my neck on the line and aiding helpless animals was one of them.

A low growl rumbled behind me.

Okay, aiding not-so-helpless animals too.

"All good here. Sounds like 3B made the most of happy hour earlier." I tried to shut the door but Mona was quicker than she looked and wedged a wide shoe in the gap before I could manage.

"Would you mind if I took a look around? It isn't that I don't trust you. It's just that I'd like to tell the tenant that I inspected the premises personally."

"I would love to give you the grand tour." I made a show of yawning. "But I am bone tired and I have an early day tomorrow. All I want to do now is take a bath and head to bed."

"I completely understand. I had a warm cup of tea when his complaint came through. It will be cold by the time I get back to the first floor." She grimaced. "There's nothing worse than cold tea."

Try accidentally swallowing the splattered guts of a basilisk.

"Why don't you go back to your flat and I'll handle 3B?"

Mona shook her head. "Would that I could. I have a reputation to uphold, you see. If the tenants start to think I can't do my job, I'll no longer have one. Do you see how that works?"

I was wasting valuable bath time. "Give me one second to tidy up. I've left out a few unmentionables that I was considering for a date."

I knew the mention of unmentionables would cause Mona to clutch her pearls.

"Yes, of course," she said. Her gaze dropped right to the floor.

I closed the door and ushered the animals to the window. There wasn't time to perform the spell for the holiday home. I'd have to rely on them behaving on the balcony for the five minutes it took Mona to search the flat. We'd done this drill enough times that the animals understood the urgency and obeyed my instructions.

Ever so quietly I closed the window and pushed a chest of drawers in front of it. Mona had no idea how strong I was and would assume I'd need help to move such a formidable piece of furniture.

There was no sign of Trio, not that I could fit her on the balcony with the others anyway. She had no experience on the top floor of a building. What if she fell? I'd never forgive myself.

Where could she be? I sent her a mental message, injecting a sense of danger, and hoped the dog understood. It was one thing to establish a rapport. It was quite another to develop complex communication. Barnaby and I had spent years perfecting our dynamic. The raven had practically evolved into an extension of me.

I hurried back to the door and widened the gap and stepped aside to let her pass. I felt for Mona. It couldn't be easy being human in this world. It wasn't easy being me either, but at least I had advantages humans could only dream of.

The older woman stretched her neck and swerved left to right. She reminded me of photos of giraffes I'd seen as a child. They'd gone extinct along with a host of other animals at the start of the Eternal Night.

She gestured to the bedroom. "May I?"

"Feel free." My heart thumped as I trailed behind her. What was the worst that could happen if she discovered a three-headed dog in my flat?

I would be homeless, along with the menagerie.

That would be pretty bad.

The closet door was ajar and I inched over for a peek. No sign of the dog, not that she could've squeezed in there anyway. My closet was more like a deep bookshelf.

Bless her cotton socks, Mona actually got down on her hands and knees to check under the bed. With her backside in the air and her glasses sliding down her nose, she looked ridiculous.

I took the opportunity to scan the room for Trio. My heart beat faster. Where could an enormous three-headed dog hide? There were no drapes to shield her. No large pieces of furniture to hide behind.

A hiss prompted Mona to shuffle backward.

"You found Hera's hiding spot," I said. "She doesn't like strangers." Can't say I blamed her either.

"You're only supposed to have one pet," Mona said, using the bed for support as she pulled herself to her feet.

"I have one. Hera."

"I spotted multiple bowls in the kitchen."

Sneaky Mona. She was more astute than she looked.

"Those are all for Hera. Wet food, Dry food. Water."

"Your cat eats better than most people I know."

I couldn't decide whether that was good or bad in Mona's estimation. As stealthily as I could, I peered into the hallway.

Where was Trio? I had a sudden vision of the dog digging a hole straight through my floor to the flat below.

Mona dusted off her hands. "I'm sorry to have bothered you. I'll let 3B know he was mistaken."

"Thank you for being such a thorough landlord."

Mona beamed at me like I'd handed her a trophy. "You're too kind, London."

I escorted her to the door, careful not to walk too quickly

and reveal my eagerness to be rid of her. "Have a wonderful evening."

"And you."

I shut the door behind her and sagged against it. I thought Trio might magically appear in the living room. When that didn't happen I searched the flat. I moved the chest to its original spot and opened the window to let the others inside. Sandy growled as he brushed past me to communicate his displeasure.

Trio still hadn't materialized. Maybe she'd been summoned from another realm and had managed to find her way back. It wouldn't surprise me to learn there was a portal straight to the underworld that opened in my flat.

My bones ached. It had been a long day and the bathtub called to me. A quick dip and then I'd search again for Trio. I'd perform a locator spell if I had to, although those were unreliable and risky. If I got caught, I'd have to show I was searching on behalf of a client. If only Davina wasn't a vampire, then I could try a locator spell for her. Then again, if it were that easy, the family wouldn't have hired a knight. They probably had a witch on retainer for spells of that nature. You couldn't always smite your enemies with a vampire army.

Except they didn't want anyone to know Davina was missing, which was interesting given the queen's lack of concern. Either way House Lewis didn't want word to get out that they'd lost control of their daughter. Davina had either left of her own free will or was taken and both options showed the House in a bad light. And House Lewis was very concerned with appearances. The moment your enemies sensed weakness, they'd begin to move against you.

Maybe in the case of House Lewis they already had.

Stripping off my shirt, I walked into the bathroom and

stopped short. Three heads stared back at me from the bathtub. Trio sat in the water, bubbles clinging to her fur.

I heaved a sigh. "I guess you need it more than I do."

I put the shirt on again and kneeled beside the tub. "At least you'll smell amazing when I take you back to the Circus tomorrow."

And what kind of monster would object to a three-headed dog with a rosewater scent?

8

I decided to start my investigation for House Lewis at the smithy. If anyone could identify the strange metal, it was Lann. I'd known the dwarf since I was a teenager and I trusted his judgment as well as his forging skills. Half the blades I owned were Lann's handiwork.

Before I left my flat, I performed the spell to transport the members of the menagerie to the small realm I'd dubbed 'the holiday home' to make it sound more hospitable. It wasn't a realm like this one. It was outside of time and space as we knew it and the animals didn't exist in quite the same way while they were there. It was more of a short period of stasis, but at least they wouldn't need food or water while they were stuck there. I opted not to send Trio. There was no telling how she would react to her first visit at the holiday home. Instead I gave her detailed instructions to return to the Pavilion and sent a message to the knights to look out for the dog's return.

Once the animals were sorted, I headed toward Camden where the smithy was located. Camden hadn't fared well during the Eternal Night. There didn't seem to be a rhyme or reason as to which sections of the city were hit the hardest. Some academics claimed it was the location of this area in relation to the shifting tectonic plates. Most of the streets were reduced to rubble long ago and no trains ran due north from Euston, St. Pancras, or King's Cross. If you wanted to travel north of the city, you had to find a way around Camden—usually by traveling from Marylebone to the west or Highbury & Islington to the east. As a result, Camden was written off as unsalvageable, until eventually a few brave souls decided to take their chances. The changed state of the world led to a decrease in guns, which proved ineffective against vampires and monsters, and a rise in more traditional weapons like swords and daggers, and who better to provide those than a skilled blacksmith? Lann learned the trade from his father and grandfather and soon he'd have his own son join the smithy as an apprentice. As far as I was concerned, there wasn't a more talented blacksmith in the city.

I walked past a row of shops and paused to admire a display of necklaces, each piece set on its own pedestal and illuminated by a soft white light. Magic users could earn a nice living in the retail sector through their lighting expertise alone. I wasn't a jewelry person, mainly because I didn't have disposable income and my job wasn't exactly conducive to ornamentation—the last thing you wanted was an opponent choking you with your own pretty trinket—but a girl could dream.

The jewelry in a Camden shop wouldn't be expensive. The area didn't draw a wealthy clientele. Maybe if I finished the job for House Lewis, I could...

No. It was pointless for me to own a piece of jewelry, however inexpensive. In another lifetime, when I was someone else with more money and fewer problems.

As I stood with my face toward the glass, the back of my neck pricked. I shifted my focus from the necklaces to the reflection. Nothing but empty space around me.

I had company.

I resumed walking and was careful to maintain a casual speed.

Not in a hurry at all. Come out and introduce yourself. I'd love for you to meet my friends, Bert and Ernie. The matching set of daggers was easily accessible, but I didn't want to provoke the vampire unnecessarily.

My internal alarm was set off by any number of threats, but I was especially sensitive to vampires. If I was being hunted, I didn't want to give the predator a heads up that I was aware. Better to let them underestimate me and use it to my advantage.

I picked up the pace slightly to see if the sense of danger persisted.

Yep. Still with me.

As I inched my fingers toward the left dagger strapped to my thigh, a familiar figure materialized beside me.

The Highland Reckoning. I should've known.

I maintained a neutral expression. "Would it kill you to wear a bell around your neck?"

"Do you always walk at such an erratic pace?"

I motioned to the pavement behind me. "How was that erratic? I was moseying."

"Most people would not consider that moseying. At a minimum, it was hustling."

My jaw hardened. "Well, I'm not most people. I don't do anything at a leisurely pace."

His eyebrows lifted. "More's the pity."

Did he have to go there? I was doing my best to keep him strictly in the threatening box where he belonged.

"Why are you following me again? I agreed to take the job, didn't I?"

"And now I'm checking on your progress."

I squinted at him. "I don't need a supervisor, thanks. Been doing this a long time."

"You're what—thirty? How long can you possibly have been doing this?"

Longer than I cared to admit. I ignored the question and continued forward.

He fell in step beside me and surveyed the area. "This isn't a particularly pleasant neighborhood. What do you need here?"

"None of your business."

"You do remember you're speaking to a royal vampire."

I stopped walking and pivoted to face him. "Apologies. None of your business, Your Highness."

He edged closer, his six-foot-four frame towering over me. I stood my ground, even when he drew so close that my chest brushed against his hard torso.

Show no weakness.

Nostrils flaring, he stared down at me with a look designed to intimidate. To be fair, I didn't think he designed it deliberately for that purpose. It was who he was innately, the way a fish was designed to swim.

"Tell me more about the princess," I said in an effort to break the tension. Now that he was outside the palace walls, he might be willing to speak freely.

His posture relaxed and he eased away from me. "What would you like to know?"

"You obviously don't agree with the queen that Princess Davina took off voluntarily."

"No. It isn't like her."

"Then she isn't like her brother? The queen said she was going through a difficult phase like Prince Maeron."

He sighed. "Yes and no. Davina has been desperate to prove she's more than a pretty face to be paraded through the city. She longs to be more than a spare royal."

"I hardly think shopping for a rock on behalf of your family says otherwise."

His mouth quirked. "I suppose not."

It didn't take a genius to sense there was something about this stone they weren't telling me.

"There's a reason Davina wanted to make this particular purchase, isn't there? She viewed it as important. Why?"

"I don't know. I suppose you'll have to ask her when we find her."

"*We* are not doing anything. *I* was hired as a knight."

"By me, and that means I'm in charge of the operation."

I shook my head. "Nope. Sorry. Not how I work."

"It is now, by royal decree."

Was he seriously playing the royalty card?

"I can have it written and signed in blood if need be," he added.

Yes. Yes, he was.

I folded my arms. "What makes you think I'm working the case now? Maybe I'm headed out for groceries."

"Do you always bring backup when you shop for groceries?"

I gave him a blank look.

He glanced skyward. "Friend of yours?"

I looked up to see a large black raven circling above. Barnaby.

"I didn't even know he was there."

He barked a short laugh. "Nice try."

I resumed walking. "Feel free to join me if you want to

squeeze a few melons." I immediately regretted my choice of words.

"And here I thought you didn't like me." The prince caught up and I kept my gaze fixed straight ahead.

"I'm going to see a friend of mine who might be able to help identify the metal, but he won't talk in front of a vampire."

"Even a royal one?"

"Especially a royal one."

"Then we'll simply tell your friend my name is Stefan and that I'm a vampire you know from work."

"Lann has known me for a long time. He'll know you're lying."

We crossed the road to the next block and I turned right down an alley. Unless you knew the smithy was here, you'd have no reason to venture in this direction.

"Then I shall simply turn invisible and your friend Lann will be none the wiser."

Rolling my eyes, I came to a stop in front of the entrance to the smithy. "If you insist."

"I do."

"Then stay hidden and keep your mouth closed."

The Lord of Shadows eyed me closely. "Interesting."

I touched my face, checking for marks. "What?"

"I don't believe I've ever been told to shut up and stay hidden, not even by my brother."

I fought the urge to shudder. I refused to let the vampire prince know how much he frightened me, mainly because I knew how much the news would delight him. I had to make him think I wasn't afraid or I wouldn't be able to work for him, certainly not when he insisted on keeping me company.

"Will your feathered friend be coming in with you?"

I glanced at Barnaby still flying above us. "No. He hangs out unless there's cause for alarm."

He wore a roguish smile. "And I am not cause for alarm?"

I forced a casual shrug. "Apparently not." I pushed open the door and entered the smithy.

Lann was within view, in the process of polishing a longsword. The dwarf hobbled to the counter when he saw me. His glasses were round and too large for her face. Tufts of gray hair sprouted on either side of his head. His nose was bulbous with a roadmap of visible veins that converged at the tip.

"London, my lovely. So good to see you."

I leaned a hip against the counter. "You're looking well. How's business?"

"Fair. Did you lose another blade?" He shook his head. "You lose swords the way toddlers lose their temper."

A soft chuckle reverberated in my ear and I fought the urge to stamp on the vampire's foot.

"I haven't lost a sword in ages. I'm here for information." I produced the piece of metal and the photograph and set them on the counter. "I'm trying to identify this."

"You know I like a challenge. Let's see what you have there." He squared his glasses on the bridge of his nose and examined the hunk of metal first, then shifted his attention to the photograph. "Is someone in there?"

I nodded. "An unfortunate end."

I felt something brush against my butt and realized it was an invisible prince trying to get a rise out of me. Very mature.

"Sorry, accident," he whispered in my ear.

Invisible or not, having him in such close proximity was

unsettling me. Steeling myself against further attacks, I maintained my composure.

Lann returned his attention to the piece of metal. "Where did you find this?"

"Confidential."

He nodded his acceptance. "I've never seen anything like it. Would you mind if I conducted a couple experiments?"

"Will it ruin the sample?"

"Most likely."

"Go for it." There was an entire human-sized cocoon at the palace if I got desperate for more.

Lann picked up the sample with a set of tongs and held it over an open flame. The metal remained unchanged. He shifted the tongs, holding the piece out to me.

"Hot or cold?"

I hesitated. Lann didn't realize anyone else was observing our little experiment. Too late now. I reached out and touched the metal.

"Cool."

"I thought as much." He dropped the sample on the counter. "I've heard tales of such elements, but I never believed them to be true."

"What kind of tales?"

"Metal that existed long ago."

"Before the eclipse?"

"Ages before the eclipse. It disappeared deep into the earth's crust and some believe it was spat out by the supervolcanoes during the eruptions and then buried by the debris."

"Does it have a name?"

"Damascus steel," the dwarf said.

"What's special about it?" I asked.

Lann nodded toward the photograph. "That, for one thing."

I cut a glance at the image. "It's malleable."

"Yes, but not by just anyone." He picked up a hammer and whacked the sample. Nothing happened.

He was right. The fire didn't affect it and neither did blunt force, yet somehow the metal had formed a cocoon around its victim. How?

"I know you can't tell me details, but should I be concerned?" Lann asked.

"I don't think so."

"Fair enough." He admired the sample. "Imagine the kind of weapon this would make."

I didn't have to imagine. The cocoon already showed me. It wasn't a traditional weapon but it did the job.

The dwarf placed a hand on the sample. "Would you mind leaving it with me? I'd like to experiment more, but I need time to come up with ideas."

"Consider it yours."

"I'll let you know if I learn anything."

"Thanks, Lann."

I tucked the photograph away and headed for the exit. I felt the prince's presence right behind me as I spilled into the alley.

He waited until we reached the corner to speak. "Not an ex-boyfriend then. I must admit, I'm mildly disappointed."

"Why would that disappoint you?"

"I was curious to see your taste."

"You mean how I taste."

A hint of a smile touched his lips. "Mind your tongue, or I may have to mind it for you."

I needed him to stop talking about my tongue. "How did you manage to stay invisible the whole time?"

Typically the older a vampire was, the longer they could maintain their invisible form, but the prince wasn't much older than I was.

"Lots of practice."

"No childhood friends to play with?"

"Maeron and I didn't always get along. I'm sure you can imagine the reason why."

I could. Maeron was the elder child of House Lewis, the only son, until Callan was sent to live with them and be raised as one of their own. It couldn't have been easy for either of them.

"I've answered your question. Now answer one for me."

I dreaded to hear it.

"The smithy offered that piece of metal to you after it had been heated."

I resumed walking. "And it was cool to the touch."

"But he didn't know it would be. But he did know you could touch it either way."

"That's not a question."

"How?"

Okay, that was a question. A very direct one. "Elemental magic."

"Yes, but I saw you use water magic. You possess fire magic as well?"

I couldn't come up with a believable lie. "Yes. Now my turn again. You have access to information we mere mortals don't. Have you heard of Damascus steel?"

The prince shook his head. "I'll have a team look into it at once."

"A team? You have people sitting around in a lab waiting for research assignments from you?"

"I'm a royal vampire. Is that so surprising?"

Yes and no.

"Did you already give them a piece of the metal to examine?"

He nodded. "I see now that was my mistake. I should've consulted the House smithy."

I picked up the pace.

"What now?" he asked, his long strides closing the distance between us again.

"What now is I continue my investigation and you go back to the palace to play cards with your brother or whatever it is you do when you're not stalking women."

"I won't rest until I find my sister."

His eyes shone with sincerity. Imagine that. The Lord of Shadows had a soft spot for his little sister. Unless...

"Are you and the princess engaged?" I hadn't heard that they were. Then again I didn't follow royal news.

"There was talk of it once upon a time."

"Why do I sense a but?"

"In the end, there was too much animosity between our Houses to consider a union, which worked out for me because I could only ever view Davina as a sister."

"Why are you the one out here looking for her and not Prince Maeron?"

He smirked. "Maeron has many strengths, but consideration for others isn't one of them."

"But he seemed to be on your side at the palace. He didn't seem to think she'd left of her own accord."

"He suffers from Shiny Syndrome."

"That hunk of metal is awfully shiny."

Callan smiled. "He prefers his shiny with softer edges."

"I see."

"I was surprised he didn't take more of a shine to you. Must be the magical armor. Too impenetrable." The prince examined me from head to toe.

"What are you doing?"

"Imagining all the ways I might penetrate...your armor."

I glared at him before marching away. Under no circumstances could I entertain the notion of...anything with Callan. If he figured out what I was, he'd kill me on the spot.

My mother was a witch and my father was a vampire, which made me the one species vampires feared.

A dhampir.

My mother took no chances when it came to hiding my identity. I once asked her why she didn't terminate me, knowing the difficulties ahead. She offered a single-word answer. Love. It was the only time I ever saw her cry. Whoever my father was, he didn't know I existed. She refused to even tell me his name for my own safety. She'd cut off contact with him the moment she discovered she was pregnant. Too dangerous. Dhampirs who managed to survive were executed upon discovery, no justification required. Vampires were in charge and the law stated no dhampirs. Most vampires stuck to procreating with their own kind to avoid the issue and promote the dominance of their species. On rare occasions one slipped through and, on even rarer occasions, one slipped through with power that rivaled their own.

I was pretty darn rare.

9

I took a bus from Euston and disembarked at Charing Cross. I cast a wary eye at the Thames. You never knew what creatures you might encounter at any body of water, but the Thames was notorious for producing monsters that no one had ever seen before, likely due to its connection to the North Sea.

The surface of the water lay flat today. No suspicious ripples or strange glows. The color was its usual sludge brown.

Barnaby swooped down to rest on a nearby fence and cawed.

"I don't see anything either."

Satisfied there were no immediate threats, the raven took to the skies. I turned and walked northeast to the excavation site. This had once been the site of one of the most famous churches in the country—St. Paul's Cathedral. It had been the target of frequent attacks during the rise of the vampires and eventually succumbed to its wounds. After Britannia took the throne, she ordered the destruction of all churches in her territory. The only one she spared was

Westminster Abbey because allegedly she was a fan of the author Charles Dickens who was buried there.

Lights were directed at a specific area and I spotted two people on their knees in close proximity to each other, scraping at the earth with a set of tools. It occurred to me they might not know what happened to their colleague.

Great. Now I was the bearer of bad news on top of everything else.

The man looked up and our eyes met. I offered a friendly wave to offset my very unfriendly appearance. When you showed up at a strange place armed to the teeth and wearing magical armor, it was best to put the others at ease straight away.

The other worker stumbled to her feet and dusted off her knees. She appeared much younger than her companion. Her hair was the same sludge-brown color of the river and she wore specialty goggles. Her plain clothes were designed for dirty work. She clenched a chisel in her hand.

"Hi, sorry to interrupt. I was hoping to talk to you about one of your colleagues."

The older man shifted the goggles to rest on the top of his head. "Are you talking about Maria?"

"Yes."

His forehead wrinkled. "It isn't bad news, is it? She hasn't shown up for work in two days. I stopped by to check on her, but she wasn't there." He wiped his hand on his trousers and offered it to me. "Apologies. Where are my manners? I'm Dashiell and this is my intern, Lucy."

"London Hayes, Knight of Boudica."

Lucy's eyes widened. "There's a knight searching for Maria?"

My stomach tightened. This part never got easier. "I'm afraid Maria has already been found."

Two shocked faces stared back at me.

"Found?" Lucy echoed. "You mean...?"

I nodded. "I'm sorry."

Dashiell was the first to recover. "I didn't know her terribly well, but still. Dreadful news. What happened?"

"That's still under investigation." I refrained from telling them about the molten casket.

Dashiell's brow furrowed. "Why send a knight to tell us? Who would even send you on her behalf?"

"I wasn't sent to deliver the news. I'm here about a stone that you uncovered at this location."

The duo exchanged blank looks.

"Could you describe the stone?" Lucy asked. "As you can imagine, we've found quite a lot of them here."

If only. The queen's description left much to the imagination.

"I have very limited information. It's the size of a brick, beige coloring, and marked with a symbol."

"What does the symbol look like?" Lucy asked.

"I wasn't given any more than that."

Dashiell regarded me. "Do you know anything about the church that once stood here?"

He reminded me of my mother, eager to impart knowledge at every opportunity. Even if I hadn't known he was in charge of interns at an excavation site, I would've pegged him for a university professor or a teacher.

"St. Paul's Cathedral," I said. "It was an Anglican cathedral that served as the head church of the London diocese."

Respect shone in his eyes. "Very good. You'd be surprised how many people don't know local human history. Then again, with a name like London, I expect your parents didn't fall into that category of ignorance." He swept an arm wide. "Where we now stand was once the highest point in the City of London before the Eternal Night began."

"It isn't the highest point anymore?" I asked.

Dashiell shook his head. "Not anymore. That honor now belongs to Tower Hill. The ground shifted many times during the early days of the Great Eruption."

I glanced around. "I can't imagine this area being very high."

Dashiell smiled. "It wasn't. You must remember the actual City of London was quite small and flat so it was no great feat to be the highest. Greater London, what we now know as Britannia City, would have included areas much higher than this."

"In that context, Westerham Heights is still the highest point of land." Lucy beamed with pride, clearly pleased to have added value to the discussion. "I'm writing my thesis on the function of space and rituals in ancient Britannia, you see. Much importance was placed on the right location. Proximity to the heavens was often a crucial factor."

"You must be highly sought-after on trivia night," I said.

Her smile intensified. "My team are reigning champions."

Dashiell sniffed. "Thank you for that informative detour, Lucy."

Oomph. An academic smackdown.

He turned back to me. "What remained of St. Paul's was mostly taken to be used for other buildings at the time of its destruction, leaving this an empty lot," Dashiell continued. "It still took us years to get approval for the excavation though."

"If most of the building materials were taken years ago, what are you looking for now?" I asked.

"According to research, the church held valuable possessions that were never recovered after its destruction. There's a chance they were inadvertently taken along with the building materials, but there's no evidence of the items appearing elsewhere."

That made sense. Valuable artifacts eventually surfaced one way or another.

"Which means there's a good chance they're still buried here," Lucy added.

"Have you found anything yet?" I didn't have experience with excavation sites. All I saw was an area that looked dirtier than my flat and that was saying something.

"Not yet. It's tedious work, as you can imagine." Dashiell raised his chisel. "Allow me to show you."

From his vantage point, Barnaby must've taken the gesture as a threat because the raven swooped down and knocked the chisel from his hand.

"Stand down, Barnaby," I commanded. "We're having a demonstration. That's all."

Instead of showing fear, Dashiell appeared enamored. He gazed at the bird with an affectionate smile. "A raven protector. How marvelous."

"He's sometimes overzealous." I glared at Barnaby before turning back to the trio. "I take it Maria didn't show anyone the stone she found?"

They shook their heads.

"Is that unusual?" I continued.

"Very," Dashiell said. "We share all our research and findings. We're partners on this project." He bowed his head. "At least we were."

"Can you think of any reason she wouldn't have shown you the stone?"

"No and, not only that, I can't fathom why she'd leave the site with the stone without cataloging it. We have a system." Dashiell wiped his brow, his angst seeming to work up a sweat.

"Would it surprise you to learn she agreed to sell the stone?" I asked.

He recoiled. Lucy appeared equally shocked and dismayed.

"You must be mistaken. Maria would never do such a thing. She was highly respected in the field."

Lucy chewed her lip. "There was that issue with the budget. Perhaps she was trying to solve the problem?"

Dashiell puffed his disapproval. "Not by selling an artifact like it was a common household object."

"Correct me if I'm wrong," I interjected, "but I don't think the sale of a common household object would solve your budget problems." The stone was valuable and Maria recognized its worth. Unfortunately so did her killer.

"No, it certainly would not," Dashiell said in a quiet voice.

I knew he was still processing my revelation, poor guy. It's always hard to learn the truth about people you think you know. Your mind doesn't want to accept it.

"Can you walk me through the last time you saw her?" I asked. "Were you here?"

He nodded absently. "She left early, which I did think was odd at the time, but I was too preoccupied to fully register it."

"Did she say why?"

"She told me she had an appointment with a healer," Lucy said.

Dashiell whipped around to face her. "A healer? Why not ask me?"

I hadn't realized Dashiell was a druid. That made sense. Druids got the short end of the stick in the modern world, which was why he was covered in dirt in the middle of a pile of rubble. Once the mediators between the gods and everyone else, druids were historically flush with magic. As a connection to the gods became less important, the druids lost their place in the hierarchy and shifted their expertise to healing spells and potions. Then vampires outlawed magic except in certain circumstances and the practice was lost to many of them. Most druids moved into academia or medicine rather than seek employment in a magic-based field like defense or agriculture. Even healers were limited in the type of magic they could use. Like humans, most resorted to scientific means because they didn't want to risk a violation of the law. Vampires weren't kind to lawbreakers.

Two pink spots formed on Lucy's cheeks and she lowered her voice. "She said she was having lady problems."

Clever Maria. Tell them you need to seek medical attention for lady problems and no one will ask follow-up questions.

Dashiell tugged the goggles from his head and dropped his arm to his side. "I see."

"Are you a licensed healer?" I asked.

Dashiell offered a halfhearted sniff. "No. I stopped my training to move into archaeology at Kings, specializing in the excavation of religious sites, of which there are many in the region. I've retained a few useful skills, of course. Someone's always getting cut or scraped on an excavation site and we're not always within range of a decent healer."

A gust of wind blew past us, stirring dirt in the air. Instinctively I closed my eyes.

"Give us what we want and no one dies," a deep voice threatened.

I spun around to see six cloaked figures on the edge of the site. Wizards. My fingers itched for the axe strapped to my back, but I didn't want to make any sudden moves unless I absolutely had to. Not with two innocent bystanders directly next to me.

"Get behind me," I barked.

"There's no need to fight," the head honcho said. Even in the gloaming, I could see the bright green of his cloak. Mr. Tall and Threatening wanted to shine.

I stepped forward. "That depends on how reasonable you are. What exactly do you want?"

"The stone," he said.

"Bad news, friends," I said. "The stone isn't here and we don't know where it is." If the wizards didn't have the stone, that likely meant they didn't kill Maria.

The Green Wizard gave me an appraising look. "You're a knight."

"Congratulations. Your prize will be death if you threaten me again."

He lowered his hood to reveal a shaved head with a yellow sun tattooed on the top. Interesting placement.

"Are you authorized to use magic?" I asked, brandishing my axe, affectionately known as Babe. "Because I am."

"We do not follow the rules of vampires," he said. He snapped his fingers, prompting his five friends to lower their hoods.

"Now it's a party instead of a date," I said. I craned my neck to look at the two archeologists. "Go!"

A golden lasso lashed out and grabbed the duo before they could make a move, holding them firmly in place. My head jerked back to my opponents. These wizards weren't thugs looking for an easy score. They were skilled fighters.

Welp. My job just got a little bit harder.

A blast of air slammed into me and knocked me flat on my back. Elemental magic.

I jumped straight back to my feet and faced the wizards. "Is that the best you can do?"

"You're only one girl," the Green Wizard said. "How do you expect to oppose the six of us?"

"Stand still and I'll show you."

I tried to identify which wizard hit me with the gust of air so I could stay out of his direct line of sight. Air magic tended to require a direct path to the target. My mother had spent countless hours teaching me the finer points of every aspect of magic she knew. The magic she could do, she taught me. The magic she wasn't capable of herself, she found another source to show me.

Axe in hand, I spun toward the two excavators and sliced through the lasso. "Go!"

I turned back to my new wizard friends. "Now we can party."

It never ceased to amaze me how frequently I was underestimated. It didn't matter how many weapons I carried. How special my armor looked. How good my trash-talking skills were. I used their error in judgment to my advantage. Every. Single. Time.

I lunged at the nearest wizard, a move he clearly wasn't expecting because I struck his solar plexus without interference. He fell into a pile of rubble and groaned.

"Why are you wasting all this juicy magic on me when you could be putting it to good use for the realm?"

I elbowed him in the clavicle and spun around to kick the next one in the groin.

"For the realm?" The third wizard spat. "Why would we do anything for the realm? We are mere cogs in their wheel of torture."

Although I didn't disagree, I wasn't in the mood for a

political debate. I needed to know more about these wizards and why they wanted the stone.

I hooked one arm around a wizard's neck and pulled him in front of me as a shield.

"Hold your fire," he yelled.

I squeezed. "Why is the stone so important to you?"

"It is to be our salvation," he choked.

"That's a lot of pressure on one little stone." The ground rumbled below me as another wizard tried to carve a line of earth between my feet to throw me off balance. Fancy.

Remnants of the cathedral tipped into the crevice.

My magic bucked inside me like an angry stallion, desperate to run free. Nope. Not today. Not ever.

The wizard hooked under my arm began to chant. A blast blew me backward and knocked the axe from my grip. I scrambled to recover it and dove straight back into the fray. This time I slashed through the sleeve of one of the brown-cloaked wizards and nicked his arm. Blood spread across the fabric like a crimson tide rolling to shore.

The six wizards formed a semi-circle around me.

Uh oh.

I used the most effective tool in my magic box. I willed myself invisible.

The Green Wizard blinked in confusion and I took the opportunity to creep behind him and whack him on the back of the head with the blunt side of the axe. As he pitched forward, I sprinted to the closest wizard and sliced his calves. Howling, he dropped to his knees. I couldn't hold this form for very long, so I had to inflict as much damage as I could before I became visible again.

A third wizard tried to locate me using some sort of mind map magic, but I stopped him with a blow to the back before he could complete the spell. He toppled forward and writhed in pain on the ground.

The Green Wizard found me just as I reappeared. He used a tight ball of air to knock me sideways. I hit the ground hard but managed to hold onto Babe.

I rolled to my feet and prepared for another strike. As I zeroed in on my target, a soft wing brushed against my neck and I shivered. I turned expecting to see Barnaby.

Instead a butterfly landed on my shoulder. Its wings were decorated with a brilliant shade of green I instantly recognized.

Shit.

The butterfly shot forward and a vampire erupted from the delicate creature. The wizards drew back.

"Surprise. I invited a friend," I said. "Hope you don't mind the extra mouth to feed."

A mass of corded muscle and sharp fangs launched itself at the nearest wizard. Together they toppled over and I heard a crunch as the vampire's fangs hit bone. He quickly moved on to the next wizard, who released a ball of fire at the vampire. Callan shook it off like a ball of dust and then broke the wizard's neck.

Swallowing my revulsion, I focused on the Green Wizard.

"Who are you?" I demanded.

He said nothing, his eyes pinned on his falling comrades. One by one the wizards succumbed to the Demon of House Duncan.

His bony fingers shook as they curled around a pendant that hung around his neck. A final prayer to the gods, perhaps?

The Highland Reckoning came to stand beside me.

"Why don't I take him to see the Royal Inquisitor?"

The wizard's mouth formed a thin line. He knew as well as I did what that meant. Torture. I'd never known anyone to return from a visit to the Royal Inquisitor. They were either killed or the person who left the chamber wasn't the same one who entered. Their scars ran too deep to see.

Whatever this wizard's motivation was for attacking us, I couldn't bring myself to subject him to the R.I.

"This is my job, Your Highness. Why don't you let me handle it?"

The wizard's eyes bulged as he strained to speak. "Yes, listen to the wise young lady."

I twisted to face the prince. "See? He thinks you should submit to me." I turned back to the wizard and saw only empty air. "What the devil?" I swiveled left and right in search of him.

The prince scratched the back of his neck. "Huh. He teleported. How about that?"

That must've been what he'd worn around his neck. Some kind of teleportation talisman.

"He must've used every last shred of energy he possessed to trigger that spell," the prince said.

"Can you blame him? It was his only exit strategy at this point."

"Any idea who they were?"

I shook my head. "Wizards on the hunt for the stone."

He gazed at the five corpses that littered the ground. "Only one left now. I'll take those odds."

I highly doubted there were only six wizards in the Green Wizard's cadre. They were too well trained. Too slick. I kept my assessment to myself though. I had no interest in sharing any more than necessary with the Lord of Shadows. One wrong move and I could find myself in the chamber staring into the eyes of the Royal Inquisitor—or worse.

"What is it?" he prompted.

I clearly had to work on my poker face. "Just thinking that I don't want to end up at the wrong end of a vampire's fangs."

His mouth twisted in amusement. "Is there a right end for you?"

I distracted him with the information I'd learned before the attack. That Maria had unearthed a stone that she decided not to share with her colleagues, smuggled it off-site and showed it to a known dealer, and then agreed to sell it. I wondered whether it had been a spur-of-the-moment decision—a plan she devised when she set eyes on the stone—or whether she knew what the stone was and that she might find it here at the outset.

"A thief and a group of wizards practicing illegal magic in the city," the prince mused. "Who knew this job would become so interesting?"

The wizards had to know they'd draw unwanted attention to themselves if they weren't careful—and these guys weren't careful. Either they didn't care or they were desperate. My money was on desperate—but why? I needed to know more about this stone and why enough people seemed to know about it to already cause carnage.

"You can turn invisible," the prince said. He wore an inscrutable expression.

I swallowed the lump in my throat and put on air of bravado. "Congratulations. You don't need glasses."

"How?"

"Because your eyesight is good."

He narrowed his eyes as if to say 'you know what I mean.'

I rested the handle of my axe on my shoulder. "I can't possibly be the first witch you've ever met."

"I never met a witch that could turn invisible."

"It's magic, remember? Most witches don't have a license to practice."

"I can see why you became a knight."

I tilted my head. "Why is that?"

"It would be difficult to suppress your true nature every day."

I wagged a finger at him. "Careful, Your Highness. You almost sound sympathetic to witches and wizards. Wouldn't want to tarnish your reputation for being a royal hard-ass."

A smile tugged at his mouth. "Is that my reputation?"

"Among other things."

He inched closer to me. "I'd love to hear more."

"Trust me, you really wouldn't." I took a step back to widen the gap between us.

"What's the matter, Miss Hayes? We just fought together. Do you think I'd harm you now?"

"Oh, I don't know. Let me think on it, Mr. Demon of House Duncan."

"That's Prince Demon of House Duncan to you."

"I need more information about the stone. Did you learn anything about the metal sample from your team?"

"Not yet, but I can offer more insight about the stone."

I frowned. "I thought you didn't know anything about it."

"I don't, but I know the reason it caught my mother's interest."

Interesting that he referred to Queen Imogen as his mother. I wondered how House Duncan would feel if they knew. Maybe they did and didn't care, which only made me feel sorry for the prince.

"Why wait until now to share this with me? You could've told me at the palace."

He gazed at me with a quiet intensity. "I took a wait-and-see approach."

"You didn't wait. You leaped right into the fray."

"Oh, trust me. I waited. And I enjoyed watching you fight while I did so. And now I'd like you to see."

"What aren't you telling me?" I demanded.

The prince raked a hand through his dark blond hair. "Nothing."

Anger bubbled below the surface and I fought to contain it. Six people already died because of this stone and he was holding information back from me? I didn't think so.

"If you want my help, you need to come clean. Everything you know, I want to know now, or I'm off the job."

The emerald glow dissipated, leaving two flat, green irises. For a fleeting moment, I worried I'd shot my mouth off for the last time.

Finally he blew out a breath. "At the dinner with the antiquities dealer, the queen recognized the description as similar to a stone that's been in the possession of House Lewis since the eclipse, possibly even before then."

"And what's significant about the stone?"

He shrugged. "Other than it's old and has been a part of the family's collection, nothing. I daresay she wants a matching set. Something to impress the king. She's always afraid of losing him to a younger queen."

I fixed him with a deadly stare. "You're still holding back."

He held up his hands. "I swear to you, it's all I know."

"What can you tell me about the stone already in the family's possession? Can you draw me a picture?"

His gaze raked over me and I clamped down on a potential shiver.

"Better yet," he said, "why don't I show you?"

10

I expected to return to the palace. Instead we headed southwest across the city until we reached the formidable Tower. Members of the vampire royal guard stood sentry at the entrance. They clearly recognized the prince because they bowed when we approached. No one said a word as we passed through the gateway.

I took a moment to get the lay of the land. My mother had taught me everything she knew about the Tower and its dramatic history. Human royals had used this place to keep and torture prisoners and famous executions were held in its courtyard squares. I'd only ever viewed it from the outside though. It wasn't open to the public, not that anyone desired to enter here of their own free will. It was the type of place that harbored unpleasant secrets. They seeped from the stones and created an atmosphere thick with fear and foreboding.

The prince paused on a cobblestone pathway. "Do you know ravens once flocked to this place? Perhaps you should tell your friend. He might wish to gather the gang back together."

I stared at the imposing structure around us. It was hard not to gawk. In some ways, this place was more impressive than the palace.

"The kingdom and the Tower of London shall fall should the six ravens ever leave," I said. Or something to that effect.

The prince cast a sidelong glance at me. "You know your history. Have you ever been here before?"

"Only the outside looking in."

"Then prepare to be amazed. It's even more impressive on the inside."

"I think intimidating is the word you're looking for." He made it sound like we were about to tour a museum instead of the scene of centuries of suffering.

We walked to the innermost building in the castle.

"Welcome to the White Tower," he said.

I tried to recall the importance of the White Tower. In more recent human history, it housed special collections. It made sense that a treasured stone would be here.

We climbed a flight of uneven stone steps until we reached a corridor. The prince flipped a switch on the wall and a row of lights illuminated our path.

"Thought you might require a little assistance," he said.

Without the lighting, it would've been too dark to see the way ahead. I was acutely aware of the Highland Reckoning's broad shoulder brushing against mine as we walked. A sensation pulsed through me and quickly began to throb. At first I thought it was the close proximity of a vampire—until I spotted the room ahead.

Power.

I detected immense power straight ahead. I couldn't decide the nature of it, but it frightened me nonetheless. Power of any kind was terrifying in the wrong hands.

"Is the royal armory still in this building?"

His mouth split in a mild grin. "Would you like to see that as well? I'm not sure I trust you in a room full of weapons. I saw what you can do with a blade on a stick."

I shot him an indignant look. "That blade on a stick is called Babe and she's the finest axe in the realm."

He strangled a laugh. "I'll take your word for it."

My face hardened. "You don't have to. I can demonstrate if you like." Threatening the Demon of House Duncan in the Tower. Smart, London.

We reached a room lined with display cases. Each one was highlighted by a small spotlight affixed to the wall above the case.

"This level was where the former royals once housed their jewels."

"Are the jewels still in the possession of House Lewis?" Power thrummed inside me. If one of the jewels was enchanted and still within range, that might explain my reaction.

"I believe they were moved to storage to make room for the family's own acquisitions."

"Acquisitions like the stone of unknown origin."

"Precisely." He stopped in front of a case. "And here it is."

I moved closer to examine the stone. It was fairly nondescript, only the size of a basic brick and the color of sand. A symbol was etched into the face—a trefoil knot.

"What does the symbol represent?" I asked, feigning ignorance. I knew exactly what it meant, but I was curious to test the prince's knowledge on the subject.

"Immortality."

Okay, so he was more than a pretty face. "And the stone the dealer described sounded like another one of these?"

He shook his head. "Not exactly. To our knowledge,

there is only one of these in existence in the entire world. According to legend, this stone is the reason House Lewis managed to fight its way to the top of the food chain."

And he was choosing to share this information with me? Was it because he, too, underestimated me? Whatever the reason, the disclosure was useful.

I inclined my head. "Tell me about this stone."

"Do you always speak to people like that?"

"You're not people."

He arched an eyebrow. "You really have a thing about vampires."

I offered an exaggerated huff. "You're not people because you're royal."

"In that case, do you always speak to your superiors like that?"

I bit my tongue to keep myself from spewing venom. I was standing in a vampire stronghold with the Highland Horror himself. Pissing him off would not be a wise strategy.

"If you please, Your Highness, I would very much like you to share everything you know about this stone so that I may rescue your beloved sister."

"I don't typically like to share..."

"Shocker."

"But I'll make an exception for you." He turned toward the display case. "No one knows its origin, but it's said to be the source of all vampires' immortality and the one who controls the stone holds power over the species."

"Seems pretty accurate from where I'm standing."

"The stone has been housed here ever since House Lewis took control of the city."

"Do other vampires know about it? And if so, why have they not banded together and raided the Tower?"

"Good question. I've heard varying accounts. Some say

Queen Britannia fought every vampire who was a potential threat for possession of the stone."

"Including your father?"

He flinched. It was quick but I caught it. "I would say he was her greatest threat of all, so yes."

"You've never spoken to your father about the stone?"

"By the time I learned of it, I was already a hostage here, so no."

"Who told you about it?"

"Maeron and I discovered it together during one of our more adventurous outings. We snuck out of the palace together and took down the guards." He glanced at the ceiling. "We played in the armory upstairs for an hour before Father appeared to deal with the situation. We asked him about the stone after he doled out our punishment and he told us what he knew."

I didn't ask about the punishment. I had a feeling vampires were cruel even to their own kin.

I looked back at the stone. "And how did the second stone compare to this one?"

"Quite similar. Very plain, basic in size, but with a different symbol. The dealer drew a picture of it on a napkin."

"At the palace, no one remembered the symbol."

His smirk was non-apologetic. "What can I say? We lied."

My jaw tightened. "Did you recognize it?"

"No. Would you like to see it?"

"Gee, it might help given that you expect me to find it." I would die if I tried to throttle him, but I really, really wanted to.

His fangs elongated and he bit through the skin of his arm until blood bubbled to the surface. He dipped his index finger in the beads and drew the symbol on his arm in blood. Charming.

Five triangles around a circle. Not quite a pentagram. Not the Star of David. More like a star and a flower combined.

"You're just trying to show off your muscular forearms, aren't you?" I said.

He grinned. "You find them muscular?"

"It's an objective assessment, not a compliment." I pulled out my phone and snapped a photo of the stone, as well as his arm. "You don't mind, do you? It'll help with the investigation."

"That's why I brought you here. As far as I'm concerned, if we find the stone, we find Davina."

"At least we can rule out the wizards. If they had her, they would have said so."

"They clearly didn't have the stone."

No, but the fact that we had competition for the stone was a problem. If the Green Wizard located it first, we might never find Davina.

"Allow me to show you something else." We emerged from the White Tower and descended the steps. Once on solid ground, he pointed to the wall ahead. "Do you see there?"

I squinted in the darkness to see a silhouette. No, three silhouettes. "Yes."

"I could sense the question in your mind when we were talking about the Immortality Stone. You met the vampire guards at the entrance, but there are also vampires and magic users positioned on the wall around the clock. The perimeter is warded too."

"All because of the stone?"

"There are other valuables here, of course, but the stone

is the main reason. Queen Britannia chose this place because of its history. No one would think twice about heavy security at the Tower because of its past reputation. Everyone believes House Lewis stores its valuables and most important prisoners here, which is only partially true."

"I didn't think House Lewis held prisoners." Their justice was swift and brutal. There were no long, drawn-out sentences in the vampire world.

"It happens on rare occasions." He pointed to another section of the Tower. "They tend to go there."

I peered at the tall structure. "How do you know?" The Highland Reckoning didn't seem the type to bring in prisoners, as evidenced by the five corpses we left behind at the excavation site.

"Because it's where I was taken when I first arrived as a hostage." He said this with no emotion. Just a fact.

I resisted the urge to pity the boy who'd been wrenched from his family and delivered to their enemies. "Anyone in there now?"

"Why? Planning a prison break?"

"Not today." But there could come a day when the information might be useful. After all, what was a history buff if not a collector of information?

He motioned toward the exit. "Satisfied?"

"Rarely."

"I can help with that."

Walked right into that one. "Not today," I repeated.

He grinned. "Sounds promising."

"I'm merely being polite." I turned and hurried toward the gateway. The more physical distance I put between us, the better.

When I returned to the street, Barnaby was perched on a nearby wall.

"You should tell him about his ancestors," the prince said. "He might be interested in taking up residence. I'm sure the family would enjoy having a flock of ravens back at the Tower."

"I think he's happy with his current situation."

The prince studied the large bird. "Does he live with you? I have to imagine the quarters are rather cramped."

"We're comfortable, but I appreciate your concern."

"You've visited the smithy and the excavation site. You've seen the stone. What's next?"

"I'll let you know when I decide." I sauntered toward the raven, fully aware of the vampire's eyes burning a hole through my back. Or was it my butt? Either way he was definitely watching me with intensity.

"Let's go," I told the raven. He cawed and took flight, his black feathers merging with the night.

11

I didn't want to return to the flat just yet. With the menagerie in stasis and the possibility of workmen installing windows, I decided to keep working on the investigation and that meant a stop at the library.

The Britannia Library contained the most comprehensive selection of books in the territory. It was originally known as the British Library, which sounded close enough to Britannia that I was surprised the vampire queen didn't leave the original name intact. She liked to put her own stamp on places though. There was nothing like a narcissistic vampire in charge of the territory.

I sauntered up to the counter where Pedro was helping another patron. There were three head librarians and Pedro Gutierrez was one of them. Although he was the only human of the trio, he was my go-to for research. Without magic skills, he had to work harder to find information and that seemed to help him retain much of it. It also helped that knowledge was his passion.

The patron wandered toward the stacks and I shifted over to take his place at the counter. "Pedro, hi."

He was relatively short—about five and a half feet—with salt-and-pepper hair and a round face. His thick eyelashes put mine to shame. He wore a white collared shirt buttoned all the way to the top. I knew it wasn't to preserve his modesty. People like Pedro didn't like to leave their necks exposed and entice a wayward vampire. There were rules, of course, but the laws were more lenient toward vampires than other species. A witch could be killed on the spot for using magic illegally, but a vampire could drain a library full of humans and only pay a fine for reckless behavior. The system was tipped in favor of the species already at the top of the food chain.

Pedro rubbed his hands together eagerly. "What do you have for me today, London?"

The good thing about Pedro was that he wasn't squeamish, which came in handy. Nothing was too gruesome when it came to research and sometimes I required unpleasant details. Luckily for Pedro, today was not one of those days.

"I'm trying to find the meaning of a symbol."

Pedro brightened. "Ooh. Exciting."

"This is why I come to you. Not everyone feels that way about circles and straight lines." I tapped the screen of my phone and turned it toward him. "It's this one."

He squinted at the photo. "Is that blood?"

"Don't ask."

"That's not your arm, is it? Too muscular."

"The symbol, Pedro."

He pondered the image for a prolonged moment. "Neither the Star of David nor a pentagram."

"I got that far."

"I know a few books that might be of use."

Of course he did. Any other response would have rattled me to the core.

He started walking and I knew enough to simply follow. Pedro lived with his head in books, which made the library the perfect home for him. All three librarians had their quarters somewhere in the building so the library could be open at all hours. That was one of the changes that occurred during the Eternal Night—without a natural distinction between day and night to dictate schedules, some businesses and facilities began operating around the clock.

I took a moment to admire the stacks of books. I never tired of this place. Sometimes I envied Pedro living and working here, until I remembered that the downside was dealing with visitors like me on a regular basis.

I was a regular pain in the ass.

We walked along the semi-circular stacks until we reached the section labeled symbology. He pulled over a ladder and climbed to the third step.

"The most recent book is by Professor Irwin. He's based in South Africa and we were fortunate enough to acquire a copy of his work."

Shipping wasn't as easy as it once was because of sea monsters and limited resources, and that made international trade more challenging and more expensive. I'd say one thing for House Lewis, they were willing to splurge on items like books that benefitted everybody. Knowledge was one power they didn't mind sharing.

Pedro dropped the heavy tome into my open hands before climbing to the floor. "Not too many patrons interested in symbols these days, but as I soon as I saw it in the catalogue, I put it on the order list. It took a little persuading. Adelaide and Garrison weren't keen."

Adelaide and Garrison were the other two head librarians. Adelaide was a witch and Garrison was a wizard. They had special dispensation to use magic but only in connection with their roles as librarians. Adelaide could conjure a spell to find the right passage in a book, but she'd be in deep trouble if she used the same spell to find a sweet clementine at the market.

"The book doesn't leave this room," Pedro reminded me.

"I wouldn't dream of it."

I carried the book to one of the long tables and sat at the end. There was no one else at the table, which suited me fine. I disliked reading in public, preferring to be tucked under a cozy blanket in my flat, but sometimes it couldn't be helped.

I flipped to the index out of habit, but it wasn't the best starting point when all I had was a picture written in blood. I'd have to do this the hard way, by paging through and hunting for any symbols that looked like the one on the prince's arm.

The prince.

I seemed to have a visceral reaction to him, even when it was only a thought. He'd sensed it too, which was probably why he insisted on torturing me with his presence. I'd heard many stories about him, all of which involved his deadly demeanor and none of which involved his sexy banter.

Sexy banter? Did I seriously just link sexy banter to the Lord of Shadows? To the vampire who killed five wizards earlier without breaking a sweat? I could have killed them, of course, but I was trying not to. Death was a last resort for me, whereas vampires like Prince Callan were only alive because of death.

"Have you heard of a stone that grants immortality to vampires?" I whispered, not wanting to be overheard. Just because someone wasn't within view didn't mean they couldn't hear us. Vampires in particular had excellent hearing.

Pedro pressed his lips together. "No, but it sounds compelling."

I smiled. "It does, doesn't it?"

Pedro clasped his hands in front of him. "You know, London. you've become one of my favorite patrons."

"Don't let the secret get out." I didn't want anyone to know me too well. The better people knew you, the more expectations they had of you. I didn't have room in my life for the weight of anyone else's expectations. My burden was more than enough.

"While I'm reading this one, I'd also like to see any books you have on ancient metals."

His brow creased. "Ancient metals? That's a new one."

"Technically it's an old one. Tells you right there in the name."

He cracked a smile. Pedro was easily amused, which was one of the reasons I found him so agreeable. One time I brought a red and black winged creature with six legs straight into the library and threw it on the counter to ask what it was. Pedro didn't bat a single one of those thick lashes. He simply walked to the stacks, consulted a book, and informed me that I'd stumbled across a rare flying spider. He also told me they preyed on birds, which was a helpful detail considering my feathered companions. I made sure to deliver the creature to the opposite end of the city before I returned home.

"Can you describe the metal?"

"I can do you one better." Although I'd left the sample with Lann, I still had the photo. I showed it to Pedro. "A blacksmith friend of mine thinks it might be Damascus steel."

He stared at the image, transfixed. "Yes, I can see that." He swallowed hard. "That cocoon is empty, yes?"

"Yes," I lied. No sense in tormenting the librarian. I needed his mind sharp. Although he'd handled everything I'd ever thrown at him so far, there was always a first time.

"I've never seen anything like it. The patina alone...so shiny." His fingers brushed the image on the screen. "I'll have to think on this one. We can check the metallurgy section, but I suspect we won't find it there."

"Why not?"

He frowned. "Because I don't think this is a metal that science recognizes. It's believed to be mythical the way alchemy was once viewed as mythical by humans."

That news was unexpected. "So we should look in the mythology section instead of ancient history?"

"We can start in one, although we might still end up in the other. Mythology and ancient history sometimes intersect."

After settling down at a table with a pile of books, I paged through the thick book, flipping back and forth to the index. There were several pages with 'five' as a keyword.

"Anything else I can help you with today?" Pedro asked.

I glimpsed a sun symbol on one of the pages that slid past my fingertips. "What do you think it was like?"

He blinked his thick eyelashes. "Pardon?"

I motioned to the ceiling. "Sunlight. Daytime. Solar power."

Pedro's face grew wistful. "When I was a boy, I would beg my abuela to tell me stories of a world drenched in sunshine. She was an artist and she would paint picture after picture of a sunlit world. Everything she painted was bathed in a golden light." A dreamy sigh escaped him. "She was a vivid storyteller too. I would sit at her feet while she painted and she would tell me stories of a world before vampires. The world before the Eternal Night."

It was hard to imagine a world without vampires. They'd always been here, of course, but it was only after the Great Eruption that they felt emboldened enough to emerge from the shadows. Battle after battle was fought—first the war where the vampires claimed the land and then the battles between vampires as they fought for dominance. House Lewis emerged the victor in the United Kingdom. House August in New York in the Americas. House Wu in Asia. House Hailu in Africa. House Saputra in Australasia.

I was tempted to ask about the wizard with the sun tattoo on his head, but there were some things better left unsaid. Besides I had enough research to tackle and I didn't know enough about the wizard and his friends yet. No need to endanger Pedro by sharing too much.

"At least you have her artwork to remember her by." I had nothing except a few photographs of my mother. No possessions. The more you owned, the more they weighed you down.

"Indeed," Pedro agreed. "One of my favorite things to do when I'm missing my abuela is to go to the art section and look through the books with pictures of the sun. Suddenly it's like no time has passed."

"That's sweet." Pedro was a kind man. I was glad he found a home at the library instead of becoming food for vampires. Luck of the draw.

After another hour of research, I started to yawn. I found plenty of information involving the importance of the number five in religions and myths, but nothing that resembled the symbol on the stone. Damascus steel proved equally elusive. The internet would've come in handy, but it was now a relic of the past thanks to the uprooted earth and dysfunctional satellites. It had become so unreliable and difficult to power with magic that it had been all but abandoned and books once again became the primary source of information.

I didn't even realize I'd dosed off until a janitor nudged me awake. How long had I been asleep?

I dragged myself home, my head spinning with symbols and numbers and images of a metal cocoon. It bothered me that the investigation's priority was finding the stone, then Davina. Identifying Maria's murderer didn't even make the cut. Some might argue Maria deserved her fate, but I understood that desperation made people do things they never believed themselves capable of. I hoped her former colleagues didn't judge her too harshly.

I was relieved to reach my flat. The only thing I wanted now was a warm bed. I'd force myself to eat if only to avoid waking in the night with a rumbling belly. I hated interrupted sleep and with the animals in the holiday home, I had a rare chance to sleep without being nudged or kicked or clawed and I was taking full advantage of it.

I practically crawled up five flights of stairs, unlocked the door, and collapsed on the bed. If I dreamed at all, I was too tired to remember.

12

I awoke the next morning feeling refreshed. I made coffee and a list of everything I'd learned to date. It wasn't much but it was better than nothing.

I decided to return to the excavation site and canvas the area for any clues left behind by my wizard friends. I suspected the bodies would no longer be there and, lo and behold, they weren't. Dead bodies were fair game unless someone claimed them. Any vampire within a half mile radius would smell their fresh blood and seize the opportunity for a meal.

I cringed at the thought of Callan hunched over a wizard's body, although he seemed surprisingly disinterested in feeding from them. It would've been easy and perfectly legal.

There was no sign of Dashiell and the interns. No doubt yesterday's attack had scared them away for a few days. Totally understandable. The world was scary enough without your colleague turning up dead encased in an ancient metal and wizards showing up to kill you because they wanted something you didn't even have.

A scan of the site proved uneventful and I headed toward the river to catch a bus to the Circus. My phone buzzed and I tugged it from my pocket. Minka.

"How close are you to the Gherkin?" she barked.

The Gherkin was located in what was once the heart of the city's financial district.

"I'm near Monument. Why?"

"Kami called for reinforcements. There's a dragon attacking the Gherkin."

Instinctively I glanced skyward but saw only the usual stretch of bleak gray.

"On it."

I shoved the phone in my pocket and sprinted away from the Thames.

The Gherkin was often referred to as the Miracle Building because it managed to withstand the dramatic changes that rocked the city. Most skyscrapers shattered and collapsed at some point during the eruptions, but not the Gherkin. Other than the replacement of a few windows, the building survived intact which made it only more beloved by the city's residents.

I spotted the dragon about two blocks south of the Gherkin. Dark green. Spiked tail. A fire breather. Not ideal in the heart of the city.

Kami noticed me first and raced over to update me. "I only have my sword. I was in the cocktail bar at the top when the dragon started banging his head against the window. Everybody cleared out."

I eyed her suspiciously. "What were you doing in the cocktail bar in the middle of the day?" It was then I noticed her outfit. She wasn't in her uniform or her regular everyday clothes. Kami was wearing a *dress*.

"Kamikaze Marwin, were you on a date?"

Her cheeks grew flushed. "Never mind me. We've got to deal with this dragon."

I pointed to the dragon that was currently sitting on top of the Gherkin doing absolutely nothing.

"The dragon is fine. I want to know more about this date. Who is it? That knight you met at the weapons convention? The one with the mismatched eyes?"

Kami glowered at me. "I am not discussing this with you right now." She jabbed a finger at the empty air. "Dragon. Chaos. Help."

The dragon abandoned its perch and we watched as it swooped low and climbed high again.

I peered at the sky. "What on earth is he doing?"

"No clue. It isn't normal behavior."

"Has he breathed fire?"

"Not yet."

The dragon jerked his wings. He seemed agitated. I scanned the skyline and my gaze landed on a hooded figure at the top of a building across from the Gherkin. Lost in the gloaming, he was barely perceptible.

"I think I found our agitator. Look high on your left," I told Kami.

She followed my gaze. "Wizard?"

"I can't think of anyone else who could drive a dragon to distraction."

"What kind of spell?"

"Don't know, but I'm going to find out." I looked at the Gherkin. "You said everyone cleared out?"

"Someone pulled the alarm when they saw the dragon."

It was typical for any high-rise building to be equipped with an alarm, not only in the event of a fire but also an attack from flying creatures like dragons.

"Come with me," I said.

Together we pushed our way to the lobby. Security stopped us before we reached the elevator.

"No one in or out," the bulky woman said.

I showed her my badge. Kami shot me a helpless look. No room for a badge in a dress that skimpy.

I inclined my head toward Kami. "She's with me."

The security guard waved us through. We sprinted for the elevator and I smacked the button for the top floor.

"Hitting it hard like that doesn't make it move any faster, you know," Kami said.

"What about you? Will you move faster?"

She glowered at me.

The elevator door opened and we spilled onto the top floor. Chairs were overturned and glasses knocked to the floor. Drinks pooled together in a liquid mess.

"Looks like everyone remained super calm in a crisis," I said.

I caught sight of a man crouched underneath a table on his hands and knees. His whole body was trembling.

I bent over to address him. "Sir, you might want to clear out. We have a dragon situation."

"No shit," he said. "Why do you think I'm hiding?"

"I promise you'll be safer at ground level. That dragon could come crashing in here at any moment. He seems pretty agitated."

Kami lowered herself to the floor and gasped. "Peter, what are you still doing here?"

I raised my eyebrows. "This is your date?"

"Yes," Kami admitted, although she didn't sound pleased about it.

"Not the knight then." In a pale blue collared shirt and pressed trousers, Peter looked like a financial consultant. He also looked like he might have wet himself.

"Nope. Not a knight." She resumed a standing position. "He said he was adept with a blade."

Peter crawled out from under the table. "I am. I'm a pastry chef."

Kami licked her lips. "He makes strudel."

I raised my hand. "I like strudel."

"And I like badass women," Peter said. "What's the big deal?"

"The big deal is..." Kami was cut off mid-sentence by the shattering of the window. Shards of glass flew toward us and the three of us dove under the table, banging legs and elbows in the process.

The roar of an angry dragon shook the floor and I heard Peter whimper as he covered his head with his arms.

"Is this really what you do?" he asked, unmoving.

"Depends on the day," Kami said.

I had to get closer and figure out what was going on. Dragons sometimes went berserk but not like this. Something was off about the behavior. He seemed calm one minute and then flying in a crazed loop the next. It wasn't consistent. And why hadn't he spewed fire yet? If a fire-breathing dragon was throwing a hissy fit, you generally felt the heat.

"Stay here," I ordered.

Peter's eyes grew round. "Like right here?"

"No. You should evacuate like everybody else," Kami urged. "The adults have work to do."

Peter hurried away, tripping over a chair leg and stumbling toward the elevator.

I shook my head at Kami before striding to the window, careful not to step on any glass. I liked these boots and good cobblers were expensive.

"Can you convert him?" Kami asked.

"He's not Catholic."

She pulled a face. "You know what I mean. Can you win him over? Use your animal mojo."

I reached out and tried to tap into his psyche. A cacophony of sound reverberated in my head.

Yikes. No thanks.

"I have to calm him first."

"Okay. How do we do that? No lullabies. I've heard you sing."

I scrunched my face at her. "That was one time and I was drunk at a karaoke bar."

"Once was enough."

I ignored her. "I need to break the connection to that wizard. Whatever he's doing seems designed to upset the dragon."

"But why?" Kami craned her neck to see the hooded figure still lurking on the roof of the neighboring building. He was lower down because the Gherkin was taller, and his attention seemed fixed on the dragon rather than what was happening in the cocktail bar.

"Good question. Let's see if I can find out." Unfortunately, that meant getting up close and personal with Mr. Dragon.

Kami seemed to read my mind. "Be careful. Don't go throwing debris around. Peter's down there now. He could get hurt."

I looked at her askance. "I didn't think you liked him."

"I don't, but that would be some seriously bad juju if he dies on a date with me. I don't want a reputation."

I suppressed a smile. "Too late for that." Rubbing my hands together in anticipation, I pivoted back to the dragon as he soared past the building.

"Missed him," Kami said.

I wiped off the sweat of my palms on my sides. "I wasn't ready."

"What's the problem? You've jumped on a dragon before. Remember that ice dragon with the shiny blue scales?"

"That was one time and I got lucky."

"You make your own luck, London. Always have."

She was right. And crazy.

But mostly right.

She motioned dramatically to the dragon. "After you."

"You say that as though you intend to jump after me."

"In this outfit? Absolutely not." Kami motioned to the outside. "It's your time to shine, Lady London. Want a boost or not?"

"It would make things easier."

She slotted her fingers together and held her hands at knee level. I backed up and waited for the right moment.

The dragon swung around and flew past the open window.

"Now!" Kami said.

I ran toward the window, jumped to her hands, and let her catapult me into the air as the dragon passed by. I missed his back and grabbed one of the spikes on his tail.

Oops.

My legs flailed helplessly as I struggled to get a firm grip on the dragon's tail. The dragon shook his tail in an effort to dislodge me. I managed to pull myself onto the tail and climb the spikes like the rungs of a ladder until I reached his back. I stayed flat on my belly and inched toward the neck. The dragon struggled to throw me but to no avail. I concentrated on sending him soothing thoughts. If I hoped to gain access, I needed to calm his racing mind first.

The wizard had emerged from the shadows but his face remained shrouded by the hood. The cloak was brown not green. Not my Green Wizard from yesterday. Could still be one of his cronies though. The fact that he was still there meant he wasn't giving up yet. Whatever he hoped to achieve with the dragon, he was still committed.

Good day, Mr. Dragon. My name is London and I'll be your flight attendant today.

I'd never actually been on an airplane. They were another product of a bygone era. A metal tube in the sky filled with people was too risky now. Too many flying monsters and not enough fuel.

I shimmied along the dragon's back until I reached his neck and wrapped my arms around it. I made another attempt to tap into his thoughts.

Fire.

Fire.

The wizard seemed to be demanding the dragon breathe fire, but the dragon was resisting. Interesting.

Why would the wizard want to destroy a fabled building like the Gherkin? Was he trying to root out the stone?

As gently as I could, I poked and prodded the dragon's mind but met with resistance.

The wind blew past us, threatening to unseat me from the dragon's back. I tried again, increasing the pressure. I had to tread carefully. If I pushed too hard and the dragon snapped, I could end up causing mass destruction. When I was sixteen, I attempted to take over a giant squid in the English Channel. I pushed too hard too fast and the monster snapped. It knocked over an entire ship with its tentacles. Thankfully nobody was onboard at the time but there was property damage which I had to repay by performing jobs on behalf of the owner until the debt was paid. Lesson learned.

Come on, wee beastie. You and I are going to be best buddies.

I felt the dragon weaken and seized the opportunity. I clamped onto his mind and held it firmly in my grip until I felt his resolve melt away.

There you go. Nice and easy.

I relaxed my hold and steered him toward the opposite building where the wizard watched us. I couldn't see his expression from here, but I had to imagine he looked rather shocked.

Once he realized I was headed his way, he turned and fled.

"Not so fast."

I aimed the dragon at the rooftop. *Ready. Aim. Fire!*

The dragon opened his enormous jaws and breathed. Flames streaked from his mouth and I steered him in a circle to form a ring of fire around the wizard.

Gotcha.

I swooped lower and landed the dragon on the rooftop. Thanks to an unexpected gust of wind on the approach, the landing was a little bumpier than I would've liked.

I climbed down and patted his head. "Stay."

I sucked in a breath and approached the flames. They were taller than me which meant I couldn't see the wizard.

I focused on a section of flames and carved a doorway for myself.

"Separatum."

Latin. The forbidden tongue. Good thing I had a license to use it, not that anyone was within earshot. Knowing the Lord of Shadows, he'd followed me onto the dragon's back and was observing me right now. The thought made me laugh.

I was still laughing when the doorway of fire dissolved and I stepped through the gap. Heat blasted my skin and I was pretty sure I lost a few eyebrow hairs. Never mind. They were in need of tweezing anyway.

Once inside the circle, I swiveled left to right in search of the wizard, but there was no sign of him.

The circle was empty.

The fire crackled around me as I decided next steps. Without knowing more about his teleportation skills, there was no telling where he'd gone. Some magic users could only teleport a short distance whereas the more skilled ones could teleport to another realm. Then there was someone like me who could send my animal companions to a temporary realm of my own creation. It wasn't a skill I took lightly, especially because there was limited information about it.

I put out the fire and flew the dragon low enough to drop me safely on the ground before sending the dragon on his way. If the vampire authorities got their claws into him, they'd kill him for causing a disturbance. It didn't matter that it wasn't his fault.

Did I mention vampires have a low tolerance?

I found Kami waiting for me in front of the Gherkin. "Nice show. Next time I'd suggest dialing up the drama a smidge. Maybe throw in a crying baby on a ledge."

"The wizard escaped."

Her face tightened. "That stinks. Teleporter?"

I nodded.

"Any idea what he was trying to achieve?"

"Other than ruin your date? Nope."

She cracked a smile. "The date was ruined when I shook Peter's hand and it was sweaty. I could've forgiven him misleading me about his job, but..." She grimaced. "If you're going to lay a sweaty hand on me, we'd both better be naked."

"Well, at least he didn't die," I said.

As though hearing his name invoked, Peter cut through from the crowd. "No offense, Kami, but I think I'll stick to women who don't have special names for their weapons."

Kami shrugged. "Your loss."

Peter walked away.

"Two coins says he starts running before he reaches the corner," I said.

"I'll take that bet."

Side-by-side we watched him go. About halfway down the block, he picked up the pace and two steps later launched into a full-blown run. I held out my hand.

Kami muttered as she dug into her pocket. "Stupid matchmaker and her dating profiles. So freakin' inaccurate."

The crowd parted as though driven back by an invisible hand. At first I worried there was another disturbance on the horizon until I saw him.

Him as in the Lord of Shadows. Seriously? I'd only been joking earlier.

He headed straight toward me, his gait almost predatory. "I should have guessed I'd find you in the midst of all this chaos."

Kami's eyes widened slightly.

"Kami, I'd like you to meet..." I was about to offer one of his nicknames, but quickly realized that might be a mistake. It was risky enough to insult him in private. I'd have to be suicidal to insult the Demon of House Duncan in front of a crowd. There could be repercussions.

"Prince Callan," he finished for me.

Kami stared. "House Lewis? *That* Prince Callan?" Her gaze darted to me. "Or is it House Duncan? I don't know how it works with a hostage." She clamped a hand over her mouth. "Am I allowed to call you a hostage?"

He smiled. "If you're anything like your friend, I imagine you'll call me whatever you like."

She laughed. "Oh, you've gotten to know her already then. Nice."

The prince angled his head toward the rooftop. "What happened?"

"There was an incident with a dragon. It's all good now though," I said.

Amusement danced in his green eyes. "Care to elaborate?"

"Not really. How did you know I was here?" If he admitted to following me again, crowd or no crowd, we were going to have words.

"If you must know, I was attending a meeting with my finance team and we heard the ruckus."

"You have a finance team?" I asked.

"If not, I just left behind some very confused vampires in three-piece suits."

Kami's words tumbled out. "There was a wizard trying to control a dragon and make him breathe fire on the Gherkin. London took control of the dragon and went after him, but he teleported before she got to him."

I pressed my lips together to keep myself from yelling at Kami. Why had she felt the need to disclose all that to a vampire? Even worse, to Prince Callan?

He looked at me. "Are you injured?"

I blinked. Not the question I was expecting.

"I'm fine," I said.

"Good. If you're done here, why don't you walk with me? My meeting is finished. You can update me on the particulars of this dragon incident. Perhaps it's relevant to our mutual concern."

I shot a helpless look at Kami.

"Am I invited?" she asked.

"No," I said quickly. She'd said quite enough to the prince already.

The prince looped his arm through mine and guided me away from the Gherkin. I felt like I was under arrest.

"Where are we going?" I had visions of me being imprisoned in some secret lair he'd been preparing since the moment we met. I bet the primal part of him would enjoy watching me try to fight my way out.

Then again, was there a part of him that wasn't primal?

Yes. I'd seen a glimpse of him only moments ago when he asked if I was injured. The concern seemed genuine.

"I have a place nearby. We can talk privately there."

My skin tingled at the prospect.

He kept his arm looped through mine and I couldn't decide whether he was being gallant or forceful.

We arrived at a row of white terraced houses with shiny black doors except for one on the end which boasted a shiny red door. No need to guess which one we were about to enter.

"Mine is the one with the red door."

Shocker.

Prince Callan might not be a blood relation of House Lewis, but he'd definitely become one of them.

"Do you really not mind being called a hostage?" The question slipped out before I had a chance to stop it.

"It depends." He climbed the steps and produced a key from his pocket.

"Do you think of yourself that way?"

He seemed surprised by the question. "Once upon a time maybe, but not anymore. I'm no longer a child. I'm a powerful vampire in my own right. If I wanted to leave, I would."

"If you left, you'd violate the terms of the treaty." If memory served, he was bound to House Lewis for another ten years before he would be permitted to return to his birth family.

The prince lingered on the doorstep. "Since you've been so agreeable coming here without a fight, I'll tell you a secret. House Lewis would be perfectly fine with me returning to Scotland. It's only the fear of a public outcry that prevents them from allowing it. The vampires in the city would scream bloody murder. That's the trouble with immortals. Long memories."

Yes, *that* was the problem.

"What is this place?" I asked.

"Somewhere safe."

"This is where you keep your mistresses, isn't it?"

"I don't *keep* anyone. They come and go as they please."

"You mean they come and go as *you* please."

He unlocked the door and pushed it open. The moment I crossed the threshold, my magic surged and I clamped down. Hard.

"I like having a place to go where I can't be bothered," he said, oblivious to my visceral response. "There are no servants here. No one making demands of me."

I couldn't say that about my flat. There was always an animal in need of *something*.

The first thing I noticed was the black and white tile floor. It had to be original to the house.

I tapped my boot on the tile. "This is pre-Eternal Night."

"So it is. Well spotted."

My gaze traveled around the foyer, taking in the other features. Original wainscoting. A tray ceiling.

"Wow. You found a real diamond in the rough." The city

was filled with once-grand houses that had fallen on hard times.

"I certainly have," he said.

I felt his eyes on me. Trying to use your vampire mojo on me, are you? I've got two words for you, buddy. Not. Interested.

I kept my focus on the interior, refusing to give him the satisfaction. "I've never seen anywhere so well preserved."

"I don't have the same desire to destroy and rebuild as the rest of House Lewis. My father taught me to value the past."

"You mean King Glendon." Otherwise known as the Terror of Terra.

He nodded.

"You call both kings 'Father.'"

"Because they both are."

We entered the parlor room just as Prince Maeron was entering the same room from another entryway. He carried a bowl in his hands.

Prince Callan arched an eyebrow. "Brother? I didn't expect to see you here."

The dark-haired prince cut a quick glance at me and grinned. "Clearly. Is this part of your knightly service?"

Preternaturally fast, the Demon of House Duncan flew across the room and grabbed his brother by the neck, pinning him against the wall. The bowl clattered to the floor, spilling its contents. Nuts and berries scattered and rolled across the floor and under the furniture.

"Do not disrespect her again," he snarled.

Maeron flashed an uneasy smile and held up his hands in acquiescence. "It was only a joke, brother. No need for violence."

The Highland Reckoning squeezed his brother's neck. "Apologize to the lady."

"I don't think he can breathe let alone apologize," I interjected. I didn't want to be caught in the middle of a domestic disturbance between feuding royal vampires.

Callan released his grip and stepped away. His brother rubbed the sore spot on his neck.

"My apologies. I meant no disrespect."

Now probably wasn't a good time to ask them to stop calling me 'Sir.'

"Why are you here?" Callan demanded.

He flopped on the sofa. "Mother and Father are unbearable at the moment. They pretend to be unconcerned by Davina's absence, but the delusion is weighing on them both. I decided to seek refuge somewhere calmer and more comfortable."

"You have your own place," Callan pointed out.

"Oh, I know, but I like yours better." He folded his hands behind his head and settled against the cushions. "Good thing I'm here or I would've missed the meeting. You should really plan these things in advance. You know how busy my schedule is."

"This was impromptu. Miss Hayes encountered an ambitious wizard near the Gherkin."

"Ah, I see. And you've come here to regroup." He motioned to the loveseat adjacent to the sofa. "I'm intrigued. Do sit and tell me all about it."

Callan and I squeezed awkwardly on the loveseat. I thought it was interesting that he didn't insist on sharing the sofa with his brother. It was probably a decision designed to torture me. He knew how uncomfortable I'd be seated so close to him. So close, in fact, that our thighs were touching. Fabulous.

"No new leads on Davina then?" Maeron asked.

"Not yet," I said.

Maeron inhaled deeply, as though using his breath to draw a thought to the surface. "What about the other Houses like Peyton or Kane?"

Callan's gaze flicked to his brother. "What about them?"

"Do we not think there's a chance they're involved? A mysterious stone and a missing heir to House Lewis? If you ask me, it's a power play."

"Which is why no one is asking you," Callan said.

"Is this really such a shocking possibility? It's been decades since the Houses have clashed. We're due."

I felt the prince tense beside me. "Twenty years, to be precise," he said. "There is no evidence to suggest the involvement of another House."

"Perhaps because we haven't found it yet."

"Don't you think Mother and Father would be more concerned if they suspected another House was preparing to make a move?"

Maeron sniffed. "They've grown complacent."

"You say that because you long for conflict. I can assure you, brother, there are no winners in warfare."

I glanced sideways at him. It was a curious comment from the Demon of House Duncan.

"And you only say that because you lost."

Before I could blink, Callan was off the loveseat. The sofa flipped backward as the princes pummeled each other. I had no idea vampires were so quick to violence when it came to each other. Shifters, yes. Vampires gave the illusion of being more civilized. Consider me educated.

Uncertain what to do and unwilling to get caught in the melee, I remained seated. It was like watching a performance. I was tempted to scrape a few nuts off the floor and enjoy a snack.

Once they'd beaten each other to their mutual satisfaction, they placed the sofa in its original position and returned to their seats.

I looked from one prince to the other. "Do you two always fight like this?"

"No," Maeron said. "Usually there are weapons involved."

Good to know.

"I don't mean to take sides,"—because I valued my life—"but Prince Maeron has a point."

"He does?"

"I do?"

"The wizard seemed to want to force the dragon to unleash fire on the Gherkin, which is one of the most famous, longstanding buildings in the region. It makes sense that a rival House would view it as a political target."

Callan blinked at me. "You think the wizard might have been sent by a rival House?"

"I think it's a possibility that deserves consideration."

"Why else would someone attack the Gherkin?" Maeron interjected.

"It's hideous for one thing. Perhaps someone with taste was taking a stand."

"If another House is behind this, we might need to consider employing more than a single knight," Maeron said. "No matter how capable she appears."

Callan shook his head. "We need more information first. The whole point of hiring an unknown is to keep House business under the radar. We can't go accusing another House without proof."

Maeron gave me a speculative glance. "Seems you

might've bitten off more than you can chew. The question is—can you handle it?"

Callan answered before I could. "I believe she can."

Maeron kept his gaze fixed on me. "Good, because if there's one thing House Lewis doesn't handle well, it's disappointment."

13

I extricated myself from my impromptu meeting with the princes and returned to the Circus. The first thing I noticed was a trail of cotton. I followed it to the corner of the room where a dog bed had been ripped to shreds.

"What happened? Someone was unhappy with the color?"

Trio trotted over to greet me. Three tongues licked my arm.

"I probably smell like a mix of dragon and vampire."

Ione glanced up from her paperwork. Ione Sheehan and her older sister Neera were both Knights of Boudica. They were skilled archers as well as practitioners of earth magic. Tall, slender, and pale, with light brown hair in a French knot, Ione looked more like a prim primary school teacher than a knight. Like many of us, she and Neera lost their parents at a young age and learned to survive by becoming adept fighters.

"Do I even want to know?" she asked.

"Definitely not." There was no sign of Kami. No doubt she'd gone home to change her clothes and look disgruntled over the outcome of her date. Too bad they didn't hit it off or it would've made a great story to tell their grandchildren.

I sat at my desk and debated whether to write a report on the dragon. Technically it wasn't required because the dragon interference wasn't part of my official duties. My time would be better spent finding the stone and Davina. The possibility of a brewing battle between Houses wasn't ideal. Despite Callan's confidence in me, a situation with severe political repercussions was above my pay grade.

I gnawed on a carrot stick and attempted to brainstorm. It was hard to generate ideas when I was hungry. I needed crunchy fuel.

Minka's phone bleeped once and immediately fell silent. "I think it was Stevie."

"Wait and see if she calls back." Ione closed a file and delivered it to Minka. She didn't share my intense dislike of bureaucracy, but I definitely heard her grumble about a sore thumb joint more than once today.

Minka watched the phone and waited.

I noticed her look of consternation. "What's the big deal?"

"She started a job for a new client today."

I shrugged. "And?"

Minka lowered her head. "I might not have fully vetted him."

Ione and I exchanged glances. Since when did Minka, the queen of all things administrative, not fully vet someone? Just because we were the last resort for many people didn't mean we took absolutely any job that came through the door. An all-female banner suffered from more than its fair share of bullies and misogynists. We'd been lured to cage fights and endured piss-poor trafficking attempts. Kami was once hired to work what was supposed to be security for a wealthy wizard who owned an adults-only traveling circus. Turned out he thought it would be hot to have a female knight in the center ring to square off against a couple minotaurs night after night. Let's just say he regretted that decision and Kami left with a set of horns that she used to embellish the top of her favorite chair.

"Why didn't you vet him?" Ione demanded. "It's in the rules."

We all knew how much Minka coveted the rules.

"He offered double the rate," she admitted.

Red flag. "Did you ask why?"

Minka straightened. "Naturally. He said it was because the job was urgent and he knew our time was valuable."

She fell for flattery? How very unlike her.

"He also said Sergio recommended us."

That made a bit more sense. Sergio was like Mack, another knight that directed clients our way when his banner was fully booked or had a conflict of interest.

Minka's phone bleeped again and she pounced. "Hello? Stevie?"

Nothing.

"Where was she going?" Ione asked.

Minka shook her head. "Not sure. I passed the details along, but I was busy at the time."

I pulled out my phone and saw a signal. "I'll call her."

"Why does your phone work?" Minka huffed.

I gave her a sharp look. "Seriously? You're suffering from comparisonitis now?" I found Stevie in my contacts and tapped the speaker button.

She picked up on the first ring. "Waterloo Bridge," Stevie's voice crackled and the connection died.

I cursed the unreliable satellites. There was only so much magic could do to keep them working. If the magic was powerful enough to cut through the dense atmosphere and reach the satellites, then they'd also be able to create holes for sunlight. That hadn't happened, not for lack of trying though. Every so often there'd be an article in the newspaper about a secret team of scientists or magic users working to restore sunlight. Reporters tended to avoid those stories for the most part, unless they wanted to field a visit from House Lewis and a demand to reveal their sources. Vampires weren't as keen as everyone else when it came to welcoming back the sun. For obvious reasons.

Ione jumped to her feet and knocked back her chair in the process. "Let's go."

"We don't know what she's dealing with," Minka said. "How do we know which weapons to bring?"

I frowned at her. "How long have you been doing this job? You don't wait for the right set of circumstances. You grab your best weapon and charge."

Minka jerked chin upward. "Maybe that's what you do. Some of us prefer to be more strategic."

"And some of us prefer not to be dead." I wasn't wasting any more time. Stevie had an emergency. It didn't matter what it was. She called us and we needed to get to her. Now.

I secured my daggers and strapped my axe to my back. When in doubt, Babe was my best bet. I learned how to throw an axe when I was barely strong enough to lift one. My mother liked its versatility and thought it was more practical than a sword. She wasn't wrong.

I strode toward the exit. I sensed a presence behind me and knew without looking that Ione was there. She was light on her feet, which was one of the reasons she made a terrific archer. She could creep up on a target and be well within range before they even noticed her.

"I'll stay here in case she shows up," Minka called after us.

Sure. You do that.

SPANNING THE THAMES, Waterloo Bridge was a pre-Eternal Night structure. Its survival was impressive considering the creatures that sometimes emerged from the river. Sensible residents didn't cross it though. Not unless you were a vampire. They ruled the entire city, but they had a stranglehold on areas south of the river. It was where much of the vampire lower class had settled. If you were a witch or a werewolf, you'd only cross Waterloo Bridge for a very good reason, usually one that involved life or death. For a human to cross it was suicide.

The aquatic monsters didn't help matters. Like the Serpentine, the river had its share of creatures that leaked from the depths of the oceans during the Great Eruption and found their way to more populated areas. The River Thames was notorious for spitting out the occasional kraken or a school of sirens that lured suspecting-but-weak-willed victims to their doom.

"What are you thinking—mermaids?" Ione asked as we hurried along the Strand.

"Bigger. Stevie wouldn't request backup for mermaids." She was a witch who specialized in water magic. She could handle a mermaid with an attitude problem.

"I can't believe Minka." Ione's face hardened. "If anything happens to Stevie..."

"Nothing will happen to her." I made sure to sound more certain than I felt. Knights died on the job every day and we both knew it, especially knights like us whose resources were limited.

A pulse of magic tugged me toward the river. I rounded the corner and glimpsed Stevie's silhouette in the center of the bridge. Her feet were planted hip-width apart and she held her sword at the ready as she faced the water. Whatever she was anticipating, she wasn't willing to be caught off guard.

Ione opened her mouth to call Stevie's name and I clamped a hand over it. We couldn't risk distracting her at a crucial moment.

Ione bit my finger. "You still smell like dragon."

I removed my hand and put a finger to my lips. "Something's coming and she wants to be ready."

"She also wants our help or she wouldn't have called."

"She's a water witch. If anyone can handle an angry river, it's Stevie."

Ione declined to heed my advice. She charged ahead and I groaned in exasperation. What was she thinking? I was the one who went running into the fray against the advice of others. Ione was usually more thoughtful.

Black waves chopped across the surface but there was no wind. Stevie was right. Something was coming.

I started toward her. Stevie's feet were cemented on the bridge and Ione was halfway to her when the water rose up and twisted itself into a funnel. It had to be ten feet in circumference. And it was heading straight for the bridge.

I broke into a run.

The funnel spun across the bridge and captured Stevie in its spout.

"No!"

The funnel swept over the bridge and continued to the other side of the river. There was no sign of Stevie, not in the funnel or in the river.

Ione leaned over the railing and scanned the water. The

funnel spun along the surface of the river like a whirling dervish with the waves bobbing up and down around it like supplicants.

"I've never seen anything like it," Ione said. Her fingers looked like they itched to reach for her bow, but she seemed to recognize the futility of that particular weapon.

Water witch or not, if we didn't get Stevie out of there soon, she would drown.

The waterspout continued to spin across the river in a haphazard fashion. There didn't seem to be any rhyme or reason to the movement.

I inhaled sharply when I saw two hands break through the wall of water. Stevie dove headfirst into the river. The funnel splashed over the side and soaked the pavement before flattening again.

What the hell?

Stevie swam to the north side and crawled to safety. Ione and I bolted from the bridge.

This wasn't a natural event. Even without the telltale sign of magical energy humming in the air, water didn't rise up and form a spout under the current conditions. Unfortunately in an area as large and varied as this, it was impossible to tell where the magic was emanating from.

"No damage. No obvious target. What was the point of that?" Ione asked.

I shook my head. "No idea."

Stevie came into view and I relaxed slightly. She jogged toward us, wearing a bright smile. "Nice day for a swim, right?"

"I'll take your word for it."

"Why were you on the bridge in the first place?" Ione asked.

She cut a glance at the calm river. "I'd finished with a

client at Charing Cross and was about to leave when I felt a pulse of magic. It was...odd. Then another one, this one stronger. I started walking around to see if I could identify the source. Finally I realized it was coming from the water."

"Is that why you walked across the bridge?" I asked.

She nodded. "I wanted a better view."

And yet all the magic did was create a waterspout.

"Maybe there was a creature underwater that lured you there like a siren," Ione said. "Do you think the client was setting you up?"

Stevie shook her head. "Total coincidence. His job involved muting a family of banshees that lived next door to him. I got the distinct impression that he liked the idea of silencing women and got off on the idea of another woman doing the silencing."

"Minka said he was willing to pay double because it was urgent." Now we knew why.

Stevie shrugged. "He hasn't slept in days because they won't stop wailing, or so he claimed." She cast a glance at the river. "I think the river magic was more of a wrong place, wrong time situation."

I thought of Kami and the dragon. "There seems to be a lot of that going around."

Stevie shook droplets of water from her dark hair. "Anybody hungry? All that excitement worked up my appetite."

I was never one to turn down food—unless it was being offered by royal vampires.

"There's a place on the Strand that makes an excellent tofu burger," Ione said.

Stevie shrugged. "Whatever. At this point I'll eat the menu."

I gestured to her outfit. "Might want to take care of your

wet clothes first. They don't tend to like it when you leave a puddle under your chair."

Stevie closed her eyes and concentrated on the water molecules. In less than a minute she was dry as a bone.

"I bet you don't even keep towels in your bathroom," Ione accused.

Stevie smiled. "Not gonna lie. It's a money saver."

We almost made it to the restaurant. Almost.

A woman dashed past us, gasping for breath. "Run," she panted, and kept going.

I spun around to see more people headed in our direction.

"Monsters," a man shouted. He nearly collided with me in his effort to escape.

Ione and I reached for our weapons at the same time. Stevie glanced longingly at the restaurant.

"I'm so hungry."

"Five minutes," I said.

Metal creaked and groaned like the bones of an aging giant.

Ione stood on the tips of her boots and craned her neck. "I don't see anything."

A flash of movement on a nearby rooftop caught my eye and I squinted at the stretch of gray.

"Heads up, knights," Stevie said.

I turned to see her pointing at the building across the street. Horror crept across my skin as the building started to sag.

I sprinted to the group gathered at the front of the building and shouted for them to move back.

"Is anyone inside?" I yelled.

A bald man in a tweed jacket stepped backward, looking

dazed. "Someone called in an explosive threat. We thought it was a hoax but we followed protocol and evacuated."

"And you're certain everyone's out? Nobody hiding in the restroom who was too lazy to take the stairs?"

He shook his head, still in a stupor.

A heavyset woman elbowed him aside. "I'm the fire marshal. Every floor was clear."

Thank the gods. This was no hoax. The building was going down one way or another.

Stevie and Ione grasped the situation and herded the onlookers across the street and out of harm's way. The sides of the building began to drip like liquid silver. The creaking and groaning suddenly stopped.

Ione stared. "What's happening?"

"It's going down, that's what," Stevie said in awe.

"Do you feel that?" I whispered.

The two of them looked at me.

"Magic?" Ione asked.

I nodded.

People screamed as the building continued to melt, leaving only a shiny puddle of molten gray.

The entire building melted.

The crowd dispersed as the puddle spread to cover a larger area. Vampires in white uniforms began to arrive at the scene. Someone had called it in to emergency services.

I glanced at the rooftop where I'd seen movement. It was worth a look.

"Come with me," I said.

We crossed the street and entered the building. No sign of security. They'd either evacuated too or there was none to begin with.

We took the elevator to the top floor and then a staircase to the rooftop. I called to Barnaby. It wouldn't hurt to have a bird's-eye view of the area. If there had been someone up here, maybe the raven could find him. I walked along the perimeter of the roof hunting for clues. A gum wrapper. A cigarette. Anything.

Barnaby landed on the ledge and cawed. I updated him on the situation and asked him to sweep the area from above.

I leaned my forearms against the ledge and observed the silver pool below. I didn't want to engage with emergency services. Too many vampires and their very red tape.

"Penny for your thoughts," Stevie said, joining me.

I smiled. "Cheapskate."

"I don't see anything up here." Ione peered at the scene below. "If anyone was here, he's long gone."

"We should find out which companies worked out of the building," Stevie said.

"I'm not sure it matters. I don't think the businesses themselves were a target."

They both looked at me.

"You know something," Stevie said.

"*Know* is a bit of a stretch at this point."

"But you have a theory," Ione pressed.

"Call it a hunch."

Stevie turned to lean her low back against the ledge. "The job for House Lewis?"

I nodded.

"How so?" Stevie asked.

"That part's confidential."

Ione cried out and plucked a small object from the air.

"What is it?" I asked.

She opened the palm of her hand to reveal a single petal. It was dark purple in color and narrow and oblong in shape.

Stevie inched closer to examine it. "Wow. A real flower in the wild. Not something you see every day."

"It wasn't up here growing naturally, I can guarantee that," I said.

Ione kept her thumb on the petal to prevent it from blowing away. "What kind is it?"

I blew out a breath. "No idea."

"Feels silky." Ione pinched the petal between two fingers and offered it to me. "Your case. Your petal."

"Thanks." I slipped it into my pocket.

"Why did you take the job?" Ione asked.

I shot her a quizzical look. "Why do any of us take jobs? Money."

"You're working for vampires." She paused. "No. Not just vampires. *The* vampires. The worst of the worst."

"And they're paying me a lot of money to do it. I'll have financial security for the first time since..." I trailed off. I hated referencing my mother's death. It only served to remind me of a life that no longer existed.

Ione studied me the way she studied everything. My skin crawled. I didn't like to be placed under a microscope by anyone, even a friend.

"The London I know would sooner starve than take money from vampires."

"This London is bigger and therefore hungrier."

"Speaking of hungry..." Stevie began, pointing across the street.

"Is it because you're afraid of them? It's fine to admit it. They're House Lewis. They're terrifying."

I snuck a peek at her. "They are a little scary. And Prince Callan made it clear that no one says no to them."

"What's he like? I have to imagine with a nickname like the Highland Reckoning, he's the scariest of them all."

None of the words that came to mind seemed to adequately describe him. "He's something."

Barnaby returned without new information. Time to go.

We vacated the rooftop and headed to the restaurant. I felt frustrated. A single petal. That was my evidence of—what exactly? I couldn't even confirm the presence of a wizard, let alone whether he was the same as the Gherkin wizard. It was pure speculation. The Gherkin wizard had tried to control a dragon's fire and failed. This wizard wanted to control metal and succeeded. There seemed to be wizards in the heart of the city messing around with magic in a big way. It couldn't be a coincidence. Whoever these wizards were, they likely had the missing stone and Davina, assuming she was still alive, which I did. If they'd killed her, her body would have been discovered alongside Maria's. But why keep her alive? She had to be part of a grander plan.

My mind was too unfocused to form cohesive thoughts. I just watched someone melt an entire building simply because he could. I had to untangle this and I wouldn't be able to rest until I pulled the threads as far as they could possibly go.

14

Kew Gardens, or the Royal Botanic Gardens, was the repository for most varieties of plants and trees in the realm. It was operated by a coven of witches employed by House Lewis. Jobs at Kew Gardens were highly sought after. They paid well and the work was gratifying—if you were into magic that supported plant life. As an earth witch, Neera had considered a job here once upon a time, but she couldn't stomach the idea of working directly for vampires.

On the first Sunday of each month the gardens were open to the public and residents flocked to see species of plants they'd only read about in books. Kew housed over 50,000 kinds, which took quite a lot of magic to sustain. My mother and I visited once a year either on or close to her birthday until her death. After that the ritual ceased, but every so often I found myself outside the walls and wondering whether the lily pads were as large as ever or whether the pitcher plants were still eating flies.

It felt strange to be here now for an entirely different reason.

I waited patiently for the gardens to open, listening to

the excited chatter around me. A mix of species had lined up for admittance today. As usual, there were few vampires, for which I was grateful.

Once inside the grounds, I toured the greenhouses and half listened to the description of how magic now supported the growth of plants. I knew the speech by heart. They hadn't bothered to change it in over fifteen years.

I covered every inch of the grounds in search of a dark purple flower. I came across more than a dozen, but none that matched the one in my pocket.

I wasn't ready to admit defeat.

Up ahead I saw the hedge maze that I'd skipped through as a child. Life had been hard then, too, but I hadn't realized it. My mother had shielded me from the unpleasantness as best she could. When I was very young, teaching me magic had been a game, at least for me. Only when I grew older did she begin to reveal the stakes.

Past the maze was a wooded area with tall, majestic trees that survived the changes brought on by the Eternal Night. My mother would be happy to know they continued to watch over the gardens.

I listened to the excited shrieks of children as they ran through the maze. For a brief moment, time stood still. I wasn't an adult with responsibilities. I was seven years old with a full belly and a head filled with glorious information. Even better, I wasn't alone.

A woman approached me on the path. Her broad, slightly stooped shoulders were covered by an orange cloak that bore the emblem of Kew Gardens. On her name tag was written 'Minerva.'

"Pardon me. Could I have a minute, Minerva?"

She stopped and stared down her long, narrow nose at me. "The tours are back the way you came."

"I know. This isn't that kind of question."

She eyed me curiously. "Who are you?"

"London Hayes, Knight of Boudica." I showed her my badge.

"You're here on an assignment?"

I nodded. "On behalf of House Lewis."

She recoiled. "How is that possible? Do they not realize…?"

I did the only thing I could think of to stop her from completing the sentence. I kicked her in the shin. Even though I didn't see anyone within earshot, I couldn't risk her being overheard.

The witch lifted her leg and hopped, howling in pain. I glanced around to make sure no one was watching us.

"I would advise you to stop talking," I warned in a low tone.

The witch rubbed her shin before lowering her foot back to the ground. "Blind fools they are, but you're an even bigger one. Are you trying to get yourself killed?"

"I had no intention of working for vampires. I couldn't say no without drawing more attention to myself." My gaze flicked over her. "How can you tell?"

"Dark hair. Gray eyes. Flecks of silver on your skin."

"Liar." I knew exactly how much magic to release to avoid the telltale silver glow. Not so much that I'd explode like a dying star. Not so little that I'd reveal my species.

The witch raised her chin. "A mother recognizes what she's lost."

I felt a pang of guilt for needling her. "I'm sorry."

"It was a long time ago, but a mother's heart never forgets. I was too far along when it was discovered, so they waited for me to give birth before ripping him away from my bosom."

I'd read stories like hers. It was the kind of tale my mother lived in fear of every day—that I would be discovered and taken from her to be executed.

"And the father?"

"A former manager here. He confessed and was transferred to an undisclosed location." She glanced away, her eyes glistening. "It was a long time ago."

I moved off the path and further into the shadows. "I'd like you to identify this for me." I tugged the petal from my pocket and handed it to her.

Her brow lifted. "Where did you get this?"

"Unimportant. You know what it is?"

She handed it back to me. "Of course. That petal is from an herbaceous perennial plant called Aconitum napellus."

"Wolfsbane."

She smiled. "Very good."

"My mother...She was adamant that I learn about plants."

"And what did she teach you about this one?"

I turned the petal over thoughtfully. "It was banned by ancient Rome. If you were caught growing it, you'd be sentenced to death."

She laughed. "Not much has changed in that regard."

"That's because all plant production is under vampire control."

"Oh, it's more than that. We don't grow it here for a reason. The vampires would never allow it."

"Why not? I would think they would want to encourage protection from werewolves."

Her eyes darted left and right. "I suppose your mother didn't teach you it's good for more than werewolf protection."

Now my curiosity was piqued. "Like what?"

She lowered her voice. "Neutralization."

"Isn't that how it protects people from werewolves?"

Another furtive glance. "And from vampires."

The flower neutralized a vampire's powers?

My mind immediately started making connections. The wizard who melted the building also carried wolfsbane, a substance that tempered a vampire's powers. What if he needed wolfsbane because he was holding Davina captive? If I found the wizard, I might find the princess—and possibly even the stone.

"Did that help you?" Minerva asked.

"More than you know," I told her. "If you don't grow it here, where can I find it?"

Minerva licked her lips. "This is important?"

"Very."

She leaned closer. "There's a witch called Marguerite. She might be able to help you."

"She works here?"

Minerva shook her head. "Not anymore. She retired years ago. You can find her in Knightsbridge not far from Belgrave Square."

"I can't thank you enough." Belgrave Square was between here and home. The same bus I took to Kew would get me there.

"She's been known to help your kind as well."

I stiffened. "I don't need help, but I appreciate the offer." The fewer people who knew about me, the better—for all our sakes.

"Take care," Minerva said. "We are all prey in a world that belongs to vampires, but none is more hunted than you."

I fought the urge to shiver. "Thanks. I'll tuck that joyful reminder under my pillow tonight to ensure sweet dreams."

Minerva nodded and walked away.

It wasn't hard to locate the home of Marguerite. Waves of magic drew me to the tiny house tucked away on a quiet street. When I spotted a hawthorn blossom on the door, I knew I'd found the right place. Hawthorn trees were associated with powerful magic and their blossoms were meant to ward off evil. As a child I told my mother if humans had been smart, they would've planted more trees so the entire planet was covered in hawthorn blossoms. Maybe then the sun would still be shining and vampires would've remained shrouded in darkness. She'd only smiled and said nothing.

I bypassed the house and went to the backyard—and walked straight into a wall of magic. Ouch. I rubbed my nose.

Nice ward, Margie. Let's see what you've got hidden back here.

Without knowing more about the ward, I resorted to my shortcut.

Blood.

I wasn't sure why, but my blood had a way of opening doors. I suspected it was my vampire blood since my witch friends didn't seem to possess the same ability.

Using my dagger, I made a shallow cut across my palm and pressed against the invisible barrier. The magic resisted.

I pushed harder.

The wall disintegrated and there stood the greenhouse. The ward had cloaked it from view.

"Well, hello there."

I sauntered to the door and pushed it open. Not even locked. Why would it be when she'd crafted a ward to hide its existence?

A blast of warm air assaulted me upon entering and my first intake of breath was heavier than normal. Sweet and pungent scents competed with each other. No surprise why. Inside were rows upon rows of flowers.

The entire middle section was bursting with color—red, orange, purple, blue, and yellow flowers beckoned me. An herb garden lined the perimeter.

How much magic was involved in sustaining an operation of this size?

"You broke my ward," a raspy voice said. "How?"

I swiveled to face the owner. Deep lines creased her ruddy-brown skin and her white hair was threaded into a braid. Her small eyes were the color of almonds. She wore a cloak that resembled a potato sack and leaned on a plain black cane that I suspected was for more than walking support.

I crossed my arms. "Your ward wasn't very good."

The crone laughed. "I have a building full of flowers that's worth a small fortune. Do you really think I'd leave its protection to a weak ward?"

I shrugged. "I don't know what to tell you. It was no harder than unlocking the door to my flat."

Her eyes turned to slits. "What kind of magic do you possess?"

"That's not relevant."

"Nonsense. I'd like to know what kind of magic allowed you to break my ward."

"Why would you design a ward that could be broken at all?"

"All wards are breakable, my dear." The crone's thin lips parted in a smile, revealing yellowed teeth. "Have you come to steal from me?"

"No. I don't steal. I'm a knight."

The deep lines grew even deeper. "You're here to shut me down?"

My gaze swept the hothouse. I could understand her concern. The crone would be arrested—and possibly killed—on the spot. "No. I'm not here about your illegal flowers. I found a petal. Someone left wolfsbane at a crime scene. I'd like to know who. Since there aren't many places it can be obtained, it made sense to start with someone who grows it."

She jutted out her strong chin. "Who sent you?"

"Minerva." I produced the petal.

"Why not use it for a locator spell?"

"You know why. It's my only piece of evidence. If the locator spell fails, there goes my petal. The old-fashioned way is better."

"As it often is." She studied the petal. "Yes, it's possible it came from here. Wolfsbane is a popular trade, as I'm sure you can imagine."

"People use it for protection against vampires?"

"Oh no. Most people don't realize it's useful in that way. My clients range from pub owners to universities to werewolves who'd prefer not to shift."

"Any chance you sold any recently?" The petal wasn't dried, which meant the flower was relatively new.

"As I'm sure you can understand, I don't keep any records. Buyers come and go and that's the end of it."

"But surely you'd remember recent buyers of wolfsbane." She was old, but it was abundantly clear her memory was intact.

Marguerite chewed her chapped lip, regarding me. "There were several. A regular client. He owns a pub nearby called The Pig and Pony. Shifter clientele. They suffered from an onslaught of brawls until he started using wolfsbane to neutralize them. There was also a university student from Kings. Poor dear wanted to rid herself of an unwanted stalker. Young male wolves can seem quite predatory to a human." She counted on her fingers. "Then there was Rudy, another regular. He married a human and his wife doesn't like when he shifts."

"Maybe she shouldn't have married a werewolf."

"The things we do for love, eh? Speaking of which..." The crone hobbled forward and reached out a pruned hand to touch my cheek. "You favor her. I'm sure that's been critical to your survival. If you looked like him..." She inhaled deeply and shook her head.

I jerked back. "What are you talking about?"

"Your parents, my dear. Do keep up."

"You know my father?"

"No, but I met your mother once. She came to me for assistance, as many in her condition do."

"It must've been thirty years ago. How do you remember what she looked like?"

The crone's eyes softened. "There are some clients you never forget, especially one as learned as your mother. She and I spoke of days long past. Of a world forgotten."

That definitely sounded like my mother.

"What kind of help did she want from you?"

"A potion to disguise her scent. She didn't want to be found."

She worried the vampire would come looking for her and find me. "Did you help her?"

"Naturally. She had to bathe in it once a week. I gave her the formula so she could continue to make it on her own. I made sure the ingredients weren't too scarce. Took a bit of crafting but I managed."

My mother had done so much to protect me. More than I ever knew.

The crone touched a strand of my hair. "You have no idea how fortunate you are. So very few of you survive to adulthood."

"She didn't tell you his identity?"

"No, nor did I ask. Safer that way."

I agreed.

She gave me an appraising look. "I would very much like to read your fortune."

"I don't think that's necessary."

"I insist. Someone like you who has overcome many obstacles…I would like to learn more. To see what might be in store." She held out her wrinkled hands. "Indulge an old woman."

I relented. Part of me wanted to spend time with someone who'd met my mother, however briefly. It kept the connection alive.

The crone guided me to an area at the back where potions were stored on a shelf. Two cushioned chairs were separated by a small round table.

She motioned to the chair on the left and I sat. She contemplated the bottles before selecting a squat blue one. She thrust the bottle at me.

"Drink this."

"How very Alice in Wonderland of you." I unscrewed the cap and sniffed. "You're not poisoning me, are you?"

"If I wanted you dead, you'd already be on the floor and your blood drained for research purposes."

I scrunched my nose. "Nice image."

She pointed to the line on the bottle. "You drink half. I drink the second half."

I brought the potion to my lips and drank. "Tastes like

chicken." I handed her the bottle and she finished it in one gulp. This obviously wasn't her first rodeo.

She smacked her lips. "Sometimes the kick comes later." On cue, she closed her eyes and her body went rigid.

"Marguerite?"

"Fire! Blood!" Her entire body began to convulse.

Was this normal? I didn't typically let anyone read me. I'd only made an exception because she already knew what I was.

"A building topples."

Topples or melted? Was she seeing the past or the future? Would there be more destruction at the hands of this wizard?

"What was done becomes undone," she continued. "The circle of creation. Destruction." Her eyes opened and fixed on me, growing rounder. "And you at its center. The eye of a coming storm."

I was at its center, but only because I'd been foolish enough to accept the work. I should've said no and walked away when I had the chance. Too late now.

Suddenly her eyes rolled to the back of her head and white foam gathered at the corners of her mouth. Great. My future was so bleak that I managed to kill the witch reading it.

"Marguerite!" I turned her face to the side and slid my fingers in her mouth to keep her from biting her tongue. I checked her pulse. Too strong. I had to calm her.

Gently I patted her cheek and tried to bring her back to reality. "Marguerite, you're finished. You can leave the vision behind now."

The crone coughed and bolted upright. Her almond eyes blinked at me. "You're in grave danger."

"Yes, we covered that ground. Fire. Blood. Yada yada."

The crone's cracked lips formed a thin line. "If you don't walk away now, great harm will come to you."

"Define 'great harm.'" I mean, as long as it didn't result in death, I figured I could handle it.

She removed a handkerchief from her pocket and wiped the corners of her mouth. "You've survived this long. Don't piss it away now."

I clucked my tongue. "Such language, Marguerite."

"I'm sorry I couldn't help you with the flower. Perhaps it's for the best."

"Perhaps."

And perhaps I'd have to find another illegal gardener. There had to be more than one in a city this size.

I left the hothouse feeling drained. No matter what the crone said, I knew it was too late to walk away now. Princess Davina. The stone. Erratic dragons. Melting buildings. Waterspouts. Whatever was happening, I had to stop it before the entire city was in danger. If that meant great harm befell me, then so be it.

15

I was pleased to return home and discover new windows had been installed. Thank the gods the menagerie could return.

I opened the window that led to the balcony to test it. Very nice. The owner had spared no expense. Then again, knowing him he'd gotten these windows on the black market, which was why he insisted on changing them all at once.

I noticed a pigeon outside with a note secured to its leg. I whistled and it flew over so I could remove it.

"I assume this message is for me."

The pigeon fixed me with its absent beady eyes. I unrolled the note and the pigeon flew away.

Come to the library soon. More books.

That was good news. Unfortunately Pedro would have to wait. I needed to bring the animals back from the holiday home before they mutinied.

I gathered my materials and sat cross-legged on the floor. I stared at the chalk circle and chanted.

Jemima was the first to appear, followed by Herman. The pygmy goat bleated and charged out of the circle.

I apologized profusely and made them each a huge bowl of food. Only then did I cook something for myself. I was ravenous.

As I finished eating, my phone buzzed. I didn't even get a chance to speak before Kami's voice burst through the speaker. "Come out with us tonight."

"You can't be serious. I'm exhausted."

"You're always exhausted."

"It's been quite a week, Kami. Can you blame me?"

"Everyone needs R&R. There's a new club I want to try. Neera's coming too."

Inwardly I groaned. "I've been all over the city today."

"Then you need a drink. I'm buying."

I rolled my eyes.

"If I can't twist your arm over the phone, I'll come over there and do it in person."

"Please don't."

"Then meet us at Holborn in an hour."

"I want to be asleep in an hour."

"Nope. You want to be dancing with a drink in each hand."

I could tell this was one battle I'd lose. "Fine, but I'm only staying for an hour max."

"Wear something sparkly to offset your dull attitude." She hung up.

I dragged myself into the bathroom to freshen up. It wasn't every day I put on lipstick—and today wouldn't be one of them either. I washed my face, ran a brush through my tangles, and changed my outfit. I chose a purple jumpsuit that was tight enough to be flattering but stretchy enough to move comfortably. I left Babe behind, but I tucked Bert and Ernie in discreet places. One could never be too careful.

Thanks to a row of broken streetlights, the night seemed even darker than usual as I made my way to Holborn. It would've been a short bus ride, so I saved the money and walked. One drink from Kami and all I'd have to spend money on was the admission fee.

Two recognizable silhouettes awaited me outside Holborn Station. Kami was decked out in a yellow dress and heels and Neera took a more modest approach to clubbing in a tight white pants and a green top with sleeves that resembled wings. With light brown hair and exquisite bone structure, Neera was basically a slightly older version of Ione.

Kami clucked her tongue at the sight of me. "No sparkles? London, you disappoint me."

"Where is this new club?"

She poked her head down a nearby alleyway. "I think it's down this way."

I peered into the darkness and saw absolutely nothing. "It can't be."

"It's like a speakeasy. You give them a code word and they let you in."

Only Kami. "What's the code word? Sucker?"

She squinted her disapproval. "If you must know, it's tequila."

"Seems a little on the nose."

Neera nodded. "That's what I said."

The air stirred and a light breeze caressed my skin. Tiny bumps bubbled on my arms and I instinctively rubbed them for warmth.

"Do you feel that?" I asked.

Hair tickled the back of my neck. The pleasantness

evaporated. We weren't alone.

For a fleeting second, I thought His Royal Stalker had decided to crash our party, but the sensation was different. Unidentifiable.

I turned to start down the alleyway when two heads appeared to my right.

Nope. Make that four.

What on earth?

"We've got company," Kami said under her breath.

No kidding. I turned around to see two more.

"Three on your left," Neera said.

Nine in total.

Shit.

They were short in stature, with curtains of long hair that looked like they hadn't been washed since prehistoric times. They wouldn't be winning any beauty contests.

"Hey, I guess you ladies heard about the new club," I said. "That's where we're headed."

Two swooped toward me. A blast of air blew past us, stretching and widening the duo's forms. It was as though the wind itself was reshaping them. They were still ugly. Only bigger.

From the end of the pavement, Kami waved. "Yoo-hoo! Free butt kickings. Step right up. First come, first kicked."

One of the bigger spirits peeled away from its partner and moved toward Kami, leaving me with its twin. The spirit moved toward me with a gaping mouth and a stench filled the air between us.

I drew my dagger. "Woof. Somebody needs a mint."

Another spirit launched itself at Neera and she ducked. The creature sailed over her head. "What are they?"

Kami spun around and tried to kick one, but her heel

caught only air. She nearly lost her balance but managed to stay upright.

"Who cares? How do we kill them before they kill us?"

Neera climbed onto the canopy of a nearby shop. "If we know what they are, we can figure out how to kill them."

"You're the expert, London," Kami called.

We didn't have our usual weapons, although I wasn't sure what good they would be.

The element of surprise had us at a disadvantage. What was under two feet, changed shape, and could kill you with their bad breath? It sounded like a joke except it wasn't very funny, especially when a memory snapped into place and I realized exactly what they were.

Korriganes.

But they couldn't be.

There was no time to worry about their origin. They were here and ready to cause trouble.

Kami attacked first. She produced a throwing knife and her blade sliced right through the first one. She frowned when she realized all she'd done was rearrange a few air molecules. The spirit's mouth split in a mischievous grin.

Kami's face hardened. I knew that look well. Game on, it said.

"How do we kill them if they're made of air?" Neera yelled. She jumped from the canopy and sailed right through another spirit like it wasn't even there.

I jumped aside as the bigger spirit made another attempt to swallow me.

"Do you want to eat me or make out?" I asked. "I can't tell."

The Korrigane hovered in front of me, as though debating the answer. I seized the moment and ran, trying to identify a safe place to buy me time to come up with a plan.

If they set their minds to it, they could topple buildings on this block like dominoes. There was nowhere to climb that they couldn't reach me. Weapons did no damage. I couldn't think of any particular brand of magic that would stop them. I was running out of options.

"What if we trap them in something?" Neera asked.

"Like what? A giant bell jar?" Kami swept a hand outward. "By all means, if you see a life-sized, hermetically-sealed container, feel free to grab it."

I scanned the area. There had to be something we could use to contain them.

My gaze landed on something better than a bell jar.

I whistled to the other knights and motioned toward the corner. If we could lure them close enough, it might work even better than containment.

I sprinted toward the corner and spared a glance over my shoulder to make sure my departure got their attention. Two Korriganes tore after me. Two was better than zero.

I could've run faster, but I held back not wanting them to give up and go for easier prey.

That's right, ladies. Free samples. Just follow me.

I reached my destination but didn't break stride. There was a man unhooking a nozzle from the pump to fill his car. My hand shot out and swiped the nozzle from his loose grip.

"Hey! I already paid for that."

I ignored his objection and fired at the oncoming spirits. Gasoline sprayed from the nozzle and drenched the air. It came in handy to have a built-in accelerant. I opened my palm and whispered, "Ignis."

It was a risk to use Latin in the middle of the city when not acting in an official capacity, but under the circumstances, it was one I was willing to take. It would be easy enough to persuade the authorities that we were acting for the greater good. My problem was not wanting to draw attention to myself, especially not from vampires.

The Korriganes exploded in a ball of fire. I watched for an extra beat to see whether they reformed or the gasoline and fire combo had done its job.

The air remained still.

Two down. Seven to go. Not the best odds but much improved.

I handed the nozzle back to the man. He stared at me in awe before setting the nozzle back on the pump and ducking into his car and speeding away. Not that desperate to fill up, apparently.

None of the other Korriganes had tried to follow. That meant I needed another way to get rid of them.

I returned to the original site. The problem with Kami's magic specialty was that it was mind control and I had no idea whether that would work on the Korriganes.

"I've got two on the hook," she said, answering my question without breaking her focus. "All I can do is hold them in place though."

Which left Neera fighting three on her own. I glanced around for any sign of her.

"Where's Neera?"

"I don't know and I can't look," Kami ground out. Beads of sweat bubbled along her forehead. "They're strong. If I try to make them do anything, I'll lose them."

"Then keep them still. I'm going to find Neera."

Neera's specialty was earth magic. There was a chance she had them under control.

I rounded the corner and immediately saw I was wrong. The remaining trio of Korriganes had Neera surrounded and were holding her in the air, about three feet off the ground. They must have realized she was stronger when in contact with the earth. Neera's eyes locked on mine and I saw the fear reflected there. Her arms were pinned to her side, which made it even harder for her to perform magic.

Luckily for her, I had a touch of earth magic in my arsenal. I turned myself invisible and focused on the ground beneath their feet, causing it to rumble. I couldn't split it open the way I'd divided the Serpentine, but I could make them nervous.

Sure enough, three heads jerked down to inspect the ground. I pushed harder and the seismic action increased. They looked back at Neera in wonder.

That's right. It was all Neera. Focus on her.

I couldn't seal them in anything while they had Neera caught between them. I'd have to be able to keep the trio in a tight group while also getting Neera to safety.

I crept closer and unleashed a blast of air. My magic begged for more release and, this time, I happily complied. I pushed the air so hard that I lost my balance and toppled forward.

All at once the remaining spirits dissipated. From my position on the ground, I watched for any sign of movement. The air calmed.

I made myself visible again.

Neera relaxed. "I think they're gone."

"But where?" Kami asked. "We can't let those things roam freely around the city. They're too dangerous."

Neera looked longingly in the direction of the club. "We need to regroup. There's no point in chasing them down without a plan."

Kami eyed me. "You don't always have a plan. What do you want to do?"

"I agree with Neera."

Neera flashed a triumphant smile. It wasn't every day I

chose a side that wasn't Kami's, but in this case, I couldn't throw caution to the wind or the wind would kill me.

Kami's mouth turned down at the corners. "I guess this means no club."

"Afraid so. I'll tell you what, though, we can go to a pub where it's quiet enough to talk and have a drink."

Her blue eyes glowed with hope. "Really?"

"You're still paying," I said.

"Done."

"Beefeaters is the next block over," Neera said. "I know the bartender."

"Sold." I started forward, eager to put Holborn behind us. I'd had my fill of surprises this week.

Once we were settled in a booth with a pitcher of ale, I told them what I knew.

"Korriganes?" Neera asked. "How?"

Kami glanced between us. "What are they? Never heard of them."

"They're fairies," I told her.

Kami snorted. "There's no such thing."

I shrugged. "I thought they were only stories, too, yet here they are."

"Why wouldn't they have come out after the Great Eruption?" Neera asked. "There's been no record of them in recent history. Why now and not a hundred years ago?"

I tapped my fingers on the edge of the glass. What else did we know about them? Nine Celtic fairies. Shape changers. Deadly breath.

"Are they inherently evil?" Kami asked.

"Is *anything* inherently evil?" The question rolled straight off my tongue.

"Vampires," Kami shot back.

A month ago I would've agreed with her. Now I wasn't so sure.

I tried to remember what else my mother taught me about these particular fairies. "They're also healers. They can cure disease or repair wounds."

Kami dumped half my glass into her empty one. "They weren't going to be healing any of us, I can tell you that much."

"They seemed ravenous," Neera added.

She was right. They reminded me of the animals when I extracted them from the holiday home.

An idea spawned. "What if they *were* ravenous?" The pieces fit. If the Korriganes were stuck elsewhere and unable to get here until recently, unlike other creatures that manifested during the Great Eruption, it made sense that they'd arrive out of control. If you're starving and intent on survival, you're not going to function on a higher level, the kind that involves healing and nurturing. You're going to give in to your baser instincts.

Neera seemed to follow my train of thought. "Where have they been all this time?"

I was still stuck on why now after all this time? If a portal opened, where was it and how did it open?

Neera beat me to the idea. "Could be a summoner. Some ambitious witch bit off more than she could chew."

"You think those were hitchhikers?" Kami asked. She didn't seem convinced. Not that I blamed her. I'd heard of a single creature piggybacking through a portal, but nine seemed a bit much.

"Maybe someone summoned them specifically," Neera offered.

"Why? What purpose do they serve?" Kami drained her

glass and proceeded to pour the remaining ale from my glass into hers.

"You know how magic users can be," Neera said. "They only want to see whether they can. They don't stop to think whether they should."

"It would take more than one magic user to summon the Korriganes," I pointed out. "A whole coven, maybe." And only if that coven was extremely powerful and filled with summoners. Summoning was one of the rarest magical skills, which was one reason I kept my abilities quiet.

"But how would they have gotten the spirits here?" Neera asked. "They can't conjure the Korriganes out of thin air." She swiveled to face me. "Can they?"

I didn't think so, but I wasn't entirely sure. "I'll have to look into it."

Kami groaned. "What are we supposed to do next? Interview every coven in the city?"

That plan wasn't feasible. It also omitted too many other magic users from the sample. It didn't have to be a coven; it was just the most likely. All in all it seemed like a waste of resources. On the other hand, I didn't have a better idea.

"What else is there to know about them?" Kami asked. "They change shape, but they're not shifters in the same way as a werewolf."

"That's because they're spirits of the wind," I explained. "They use the air around them to change forms. Different magic."

"Then could they have been brought here by elemental magic?" Kami asked. "There are a lot more covens that specialize in air magic than summoning."

Oh, gods.

Kami stared at me. "What did I say? You're wearing that face. You know the one I mean."

"Better me than someone else."

"You've thought of something," she accused.

"You said the magic word—elemental."

Kami and Neera exchanged blank looks.

"I think I know how they got here."

Neera scrutinized me with what we called her mom face. It was equal parts concerned and judgmental. "Is this connected to the job for House Lewis?"

"I think so." I rose to my feet. "Your hour's up. I need to get home and sleep so I can think clearly tomorrow and figure out my next move."

Because if I didn't find the stone soon, I had a sinking suspicion the city would have a lot more than Korriganes to worry about.

16

I awoke the next morning to find a flurry of notes on the balcony. Barnaby stood in the midst of them looking like his beak was out of joint.

"Sorry, buddy. I'll take care of it today. No more pigeons. Promise."

The raven cawed and flew away.

I let the menagerie out for a short circuit on the rooftop and cleaned up after them before returning to the flat. I'd shower and head to the library to see what Pedro had uncovered.

It was still early when I entered the library. Even though it was open twenty-fours a day, that didn't mean everyone was as bright-eyed and bushy-tailed as yours truly.

Pedro spotted me from behind the counter and waved me over eagerly. "Wonderful. You got my messages."

"Hard to miss all those pigeons outside my window. Let me tell you, my raven is not a fan."

"I've been thinking about your symbol ever since you left."

"That makes two of us."

He retrieved a book from behind the counter and set it on top. "I marked the page for you." He opened it and removed the bookmark—an old postcard of a red double-decker bus—and turned the book toward me.

I spotted the symbol straight away. Five triangles around a circle.

I skimmed the paragraph. As soon as my gaze landed on the word, I knew. Fire. Water. Air. Consider the dots connected. Interesting the wizards hadn't yet used earth magic. There had to be a reason why not.

I tapped the image. "But there are five triangles and only four elements."

Pedro smiled. "Unless you count an ancient metal born from the earth's core as the fifth element, which many would."

Damascus steel. The resurgence of the ancient metal wasn't a coincidence. It was directly tied to the stone. Whoever controlled the stone had access to incredible elemental power and their first act was to use it to kill Maria. I couldn't let them keep it.

On the other hand, I was tasked with recovering it for the vampires. Another problem. Surprise, surprise. Queen Imogen had lied to me. She didn't want a simple artifact. She wanted control of a weapon. House Lewis possessed the immortality stone and now they wanted this elemental stone to add to their collection.

I thought back to Lann and his ineffectual efforts to manipulate the metal. He was a dwarf. He wouldn't be able to.

But I could. Ostensibly any magic user could if they had traces of elemental magic in their bloodline. The vampires wanted to keep control of the stone away from magic users. If the stone fell into the hands of wizards—it all made sense now.

"Thank you, Pedro. You're amazing. Best librarian in the world."

"I'd offer you a cup of tea, but you know how I feel about food and drink near the books."

"I wouldn't dream of it."

He thumbed through the book. "I also took the liberty of gathering more details on the ancient metal. I was helping a chemistry student and came across helpful information."

"You found information on an ancient metal in the chemistry section?"

He nodded. "This young dwarf was working on a project that blended chemistry with his work as a blacksmith."

"Ah. A future weapons maker."

"I don't believe so. Chemistry is to please his mother and blacksmith is to please his father. You know how parents can be."

I really didn't, but I let the comment slide. "This is an incredible find, Pedro. Thank you."

"What will you do with the information?"

An excellent question. "First I'd like to read more, then I'll decide. If you find more information on the symbol or the metal, will you send me another pigeon? Just one this time." I wanted to know everything contained within these four walls on the subject.

Pedro held up a finger. "I anticipated this very question and took it upon myself to gather what I could find." He leaned down and produced an armful of books, which he set upon the table with a soft thud. "I marked the relevant pages." He paused. "Well, you can thank Adelaide for that.

She used a spell so we didn't have to use adhesives. Bookmarks have a tendency to slide out too easily."

I removed a book from the top of the pile and placed it in front of me. "Show me Damascus steel."

The pages flipped faster than I could've managed with my fingers. They stopped on page 74.

"Tell Adelaide thank you the next time you see her." Her spell would save me valuable time, especially considering the number of books now on the table.

He bit back a smile. "She was happy to help from a safe distance."

I flicked through the pages and committed everything I read to memory. The stone and the metal it created would be dangerous in the wrong hands and that included vampire hands. My mother taught me that knowledge was power and that statement was never truer than it was today.

It was time to update the Lord of Shadows on my progress. As annoying and uncomfortable as it was, I'd grown accustomed to him stalking me and was somewhat miffed that I had to arrange a meeting. I didn't want to return to the palace—too risky. Instead I asked to meet him at the townhouse with the red door. The only other vampire I was likely to run into there was Maeron. He knew I was working for them though, and wouldn't subject me to scrutiny.

"Please tell me you've found her," Callan said, once we were settled in the living room of the townhouse.

"Not yet, but I have information."

"Excellent. Let's hear it."

A knot tightened in my stomach. "First I have to ask you a question and it requires an honest answer."

He looked at me sideways. "Making demands of a prince, are we?"

I didn't shy away from looking at him. "Yes."

"I see. What's your question?"

"Do you know what the stone's power is? What the symbol on it means?"

He frowned. "I told you I didn't."

"Wouldn't be the first lie you've told me."

He nodded, his face somber. "I understand. No, I don't know."

"Then you'll be pleased to learn that I do."

Hope shone in his green eyes. "And?"

"The symbol signifies elemental magic. That stone is to elemental magic as your stone is to immortality."

"How do you know this?"

"Water, air, fire, metal. All the crazy incidents that have happened lately have been elements gone wild. If these guys have the stone and don't know how to use it or control it..."

Understanding flared in his eyes. "They weren't seeking the stone. They stumbled upon it." His brow furrowed. "If those were experiments, why not conduct them away from prying eyes? Seems risky to conduct them out in the open."

"Simple. They didn't intend to be spotted." Dragons weren't easy to track. If the wizard got wind of one on his radar, he would've taken the risk and rushed to the nearest rooftop. And where else could you melt a skyscraper but in the city?

"There's been no earth magic."

"Not yet. I suspect it's one reason they realize they haven't accessed the stone's full potential."

His muscles bulged beneath the thin fabric of his shirt. I tried not to notice.

"They could level the entire city with powerful earth magic."

"They could do worse than that."

"Is Davina meant to be a bargaining chip? We share information in exchange for her safe return?" He shook his head. "No. Can't be. They would've negotiated already."

Yes, they would have, which meant...

Oh, shit.

Callan registered my expression. "What is it?"

I didn't want to tell him.

"I asked you a question." His voice was low and menacing.

Here I go. Signing my death warrant. Somebody feed and water the menagerie.

"If someone is trying to draw magic from a powerful object and it's not cooperating..." I inhaled deeply. "They'll resort to primal methods."

"Blood."

"Not just blood. A ritual." Now it made sense why they kept Davina alive. They were biding their time.

"A sacrifice." He closed his eyes and swore. "They can't do better for fuel than the royal blood of a vampire."

Something troubled me about the conclusion though. "Wizards."

He eyed me. "Are we naming the ones we know? Or declaring categories of species? I'll go next. Minotaurs."

I licked my lips. "Wizards don't generally perform rituals."

"They might if there's a powerful stone at stake and they want to access its magic. Whoever controls the stone controls unimaginable elemental magic."

"I feel like they'd find another way. A coven of witches

might go the ritual route, but wizards don't work in groups either. They're the lone wolves of magic users."

The muscle in his cheek pulsed. "You said you saw a man on the rooftop. Any chance it could have been a woman? Perhaps we should be searching for witches."

"I guess it's possible."

He cupped his hands behind his neck. "Do the locations where the elemental magic occurred have anything in common?"

I reached for my phone and opened a map of the city center that I kept stored with my photos. Britannia City was full of nooks and crannies and maps were invaluable for a knight.

Callan peered over my shoulder. I felt his breath hot and inviting on the curve of my neck and fought the urge to shiver. Even if he wasn't sure whether it was from fear or pleasure, he'd enjoy the reaction and I refused to give him the satisfaction.

I pointed to the map. "The Gherkin." *There you go, London. Keep your head on straight and you won't lose it.* I tapped a different section. "Waterloo Bridge. Holborn. They've been experimenting within this radius which means they're somewhere in the vicinity."

The prince studied the map. "If your theory is correct, Davina isn't far from here. I'm glad Mother can't see this. Most of the map is taken up by Kings College. She'd simply argue Davina is partying with friends."

I stiffened, two words hitting me like a brick.

The prince noticed my reaction. "What is it?"

It hadn't been a wizard on that rooftop. It had been a druid. Who was more likely to conduct experiments than an academic? He hadn't teleported off that rooftop near Waterloo Bridge like the bald wizard with the sun tattoo.

He'd used air magic to cloak himself. The druid had still been there when I entered the ring of fire. He simply waited to emerge from his air cocoon until the fire was extinguished and I'd left the scene.

I felt like an idiot.

"I know who has Davina."

His nostrils flared. "Tell me."

"Who do the history books associate with sacrificial rituals?"

His eyes became two hard emeralds. "Druids."

Lucy, the young woman from the excavation site at St. Paul's, had been the university student who'd purchased the wolfsbane from Marguerite. There was no stalker. Dashiell had been clever enough to send an intermediary to collect the wolfsbane that he was using to neutralize Davina's powers. My guess was that Lucy had no idea what the wolfsbane was really for. He'd instructed her to acquire it by covert means and she'd complied. The intern was simply one of his tools, like a spade or a trowel.

"It's Dashiell. He's on the team that's excavating St. Paul's Cathedral. Guess where he works?"

"Kings." Callan frowned. "He was there when we were attacked at the site."

"Yes." We might have defended the very druid responsible for this mess. The notion sickened me. I'd been sloppy and that wasn't me. Then again, the group of wizards attacked first.

"Druids are meant to be healers not killers," Callan said.

"Maybe now they are, but he saw an opportunity to reclaim his species' former glory and he took it." Give them one chance to regain the powers lost to their kind and they grabbed it with both hands, never mind the literal sacrifice involved.

Callan shot to his feet. "I'll send our security team to sweep the area. If they have to burn down the entire university to find her, then so be it."

I stood and put a hand on his arm. "No."

His gaze drifted to my hand before returning to my eyes and remaining there. "No?" he asked, drawing out the word in a way that made me want to check if my will was updated.

My magic strained to escape and I forced myself to remain calm as I removed my hand. "If you send an army charging in there, he won't hesitate to kill her. If we go in there on our own, quietly, we can use both surprise and stealth to our advantage." I paused. "And we both know you can do stealth."

"Even better than me, brother?"

I balked at the sight of Prince Maeron in the doorway. The sneaky bastard had walked right into the townhouse without either of us noticing.

"What are you doing here, Maeron?"

"Davina is my sister too. If there's a rescue to be made, I insist on taking part."

"So much for stealth," I mumbled. Maeron seemed to invite a parade wherever he went. He was like his mother in that respect.

"There's no House Lewis army outside, is there?" I asked.

Maeron held up his hands. "No army. I won't even tell Mother and Father, although Mother does seem to be starting to worry. This morning she asked if I'd had any updates about Davina and didn't even mention the stone."

"You attended Kings," Callan said. "If you were going to hide a vampire there, where would you do it?"

Maeron rubbed his chin in a thoughtful manner. "I have a few ideas."

I tucked away my phone. "You can tell us what they are on the way over."

The sooner we rescued Davina and found the stone, the sooner I returned to my life deep in the shadows and reduced the risk of discovery. I'd spent too much time in the company of vampires this week. I needed to finish the job and put distance between myself and the royal family—as far as I could possibly get.

17

The buildings that comprised Kings College were mainly along the Strand. We followed Maeron who was busy reeling off a list of possibilities as we walked.

"I would start with the King's building," the prince said. "It's centrally located."

"Wouldn't that be the last place to hold a hostage?" I asked.

Maeron's gaze flicked to his brother. "Not if they want to make a statement to the hostage."

We entered the classic, well-preserved building.

"What's here?" Callan demanded.

Maeron pointed. "There's the Great Hall."

A large sign across the bottom of the grand double staircase barred our entry to the second floor. Under construction? Fat chance.

"What's upstairs?" I asked.

Maeron scratched the back of his head in a thoughtful gesture. "The chapel."

I pivoted to face him. "I thought Queen Britannia destroyed all the churches except Westminster Abbey."

"I said chapel," Maeron said, accentuating the word.

"What's the difference?" I asked.

Hesitation flickered in his brown eyes. He had no idea. Figured.

"Mother wouldn't have bothered with a chapel like this one," he said, recovering quickly. "It's not a separate building."

I glanced upward. "She's up there." I felt it the way a vampire sensed prey. Dashiell was anchored to the past, a druid with his gaze fixed on the rearview mirror. He was an archaeologist with an interest in churches and cathedrals. If he wanted to send a strong message to his hostage, he'd choose the chapel.

Callan cleared the hurdle in a single jump and tore up the staircase. Maeron and I ran after him.

"She isn't here," Callan declared.

At first glance, he appeared to be right. The cushioned benches were empty. My vampire detector, however, told me otherwise.

I pointed to the giant organ on the wall. "Check up there where the organist would sit."

Callan didn't bother to use the door beneath it. He sprang forward and launched himself at the organ, ripping down pipes and using them to climb to the loft.

"That seems unnecessary," Maeron remarked. "Do you have any idea how old that organ is?" He shook his head at me. "My brother has no respect for the arts."

The removal of pipes revealed the princess on the floor of the loft. The princes were so elated to find her that neither one bothered to question my suggestion to look there.

I watched in awe as the Demon of House Duncan moved with preternatural speed to engulf the younger vampire in a warm embrace. She clung to him, her eyes closed, and I sensed their bond.

"Hurry," she said, her voice weak. "He was only just here."

"I'll go. You stay here." I'd be better at finding Dashiell than comforting a royal vampire anyway.

Maeron met my gaze. "I'll search too. What does he look like?"

"Just grab anyone who looks suspicious, but *don't* kill them." We still needed to know the location of the stone.

Thanks to a handy directory, I found Dashiell's office. As expected, it was empty, as were the surrounding ones. I checked the library. There was no sign of Dashiell. He must've realized we were here and wisely cleared out.

I returned to the chapel where the princes were doting on their sister. Davina now held a flask in her hand.

"We have to find the druid," Callan said grimly.

"No kidding. What do you think we've been doing?"

He glanced at Davina. "Tell her."

"He's been waiting for a celestial event to try to harness the stone's power." Her voice was raspy, as though she'd screamed for her life and no one had come, which was probably accurate.

"Easy enough. When's the next celestial event?" Maeron asked. "You're a witch, Miss Hayes. You ought to know these things."

"I'm not an encyclopedia," I shot back.

Davina tugged her brother's hand. "Dashiell told me it's tonight. There's a New Moon."

Just because the sun disappeared from view didn't stop the earth from spinning on its axis and it certainly didn't stop celestial events from occurring.

"You must drink, sister," Maeron said. "You need your strength."

Davina brought the flask to her lips and drank. Drops of red splashed on her check. Blood. I averted my gaze and tried to clamp down on any revulsion I felt.

The little color she had drained from her face and she started to cough. Callan shifted her upright, but her head lolled to the side.

"Davina?" He grabbed her chin and jerked her head toward him. "Davina, what's wrong?"

Angry red lines formed on her face and spread down her neck. He held up her arm and watched as the lines branched off into smaller ones. Foam gathered at the corners of her chapped lips.

Shit.

Maeron clasped her hand. "The bastard poisoned her. That's why he was in here."

Dashiell must've realized we were here and tried to cover his tracks.

Callan lowered his fangs. "I'll simply extract it."

I clamped a hand over his mouth. "No!"

His green eyes widened and I snatched my hand away, surprised by my knee-jerk concern for his welfare.

"You can't," I said.

"Of course I can. I'm a vampire. Our fangs were designed to extract blood from flesh."

"It's wolfsbane," I told him. "Dashiell has been using it to neutralize her. Once he discovered we were here, he returned to the chapel and gave her an overdose."

Davina's eyes were closed and she moaned quietly.

Callan glanced at her and back to me. "You're certain?"

"Certain enough that I wouldn't want you to risk it."

"I have to try."

I gaped at this vampire with the reputation of a colossal nightmare, who was willing to risk his life to save the daughter of his family's enemy. He truly viewed Davina as his sister. The Highland Reckoning was not the vampire I thought he was.

"I have another idea," I said.

The princess seized.

He rolled up her sleeve and prepared to bite her. "There isn't time."

"I need you alive, Your Highness. I can't take on Dashiell without help, not while he has the stone. We're in the middle of a university. There are healers here." In a university of this size and stature, there was bound to be at least one poison expert too.

"I know where they are," Maeron said. He bolted from the chapel before anyone could respond.

Callan cradled the back of his sister's head in the crook of his elbow. It was the same way my mother had held me as a child. If I closed my eyes, I could still hear the sound of her voice as she sang to me, encouraging me to sleep.

He spoke in a soothing tone to Davina. "Do you remember that time we hid in the cellars and Maeron couldn't find us?"

A faint smile touched her lips. "So angry," she whispered.

"Focus on that," he encouraged. "Think of all the fun we had."

"Hurts," she said.

Despite my feelings about vampires, the scene was painful to witness. Davina fighting for her life. A powerful vampire struggling to keep his emotions in check. He truly cared about Davina and felt responsible for her. The Highland Reckoning had a weak spot after all and he was currently holding her in his arms.

"Why would he do this?" Callan asked.

"Because he's giving himself time to get away and regroup," I explained. "He knows we'll stop to try and save the princess."

"I'm sorry," Davina whispered.

"No need to apologize." He stroked her cheek. "You didn't do anything wrong."

"The stone...It's special."

"We know," he said.

"You can't let him keep it." She seemed to have difficulty swallowing. "Too much power."

"Do you know where they plan to hold the ritual?" I asked.

"No. Only that it had to be performed at a precise time to harness the full power of the celestial event." She coughed again. "23:05."

We didn't have much time.

Maeron rushed into the chapel, trailed by a man and a woman in purple cloaks. "They can help."

Callan lifted Davina into his arms and stood. In one swift move, he jumped to the floor with the grace of a jungle cat. He placed Davina on the cushioned bench and smoothed back her hair.

Davina snarled as the woman approached.

"No, sister. She's here to help you. Let her."

"Don't let her bite you or she'll infect you too," I warned.

Davina thrashed under the prince's grip as the man and woman used their magic to pull the poison to the surface. Red lines were replaced by beads of grayish-black as they extracted the poison from Davina's veins. The young vampire began to relax.

"She should heal quickly now," the woman said.

Callan looked at me, his eyes a soft haze of green. "Thank you."

I left the chapel and ran straight to the Circus. If I was going to take on a druid with the Elemental Stone in the midst of a celestial event, I was going to need backup.

"The druid's going old school. I like it." Kami said, once I updated the other knights. "Except for the whole killing people part. That's bad."

"We know when," Minka said. "Do we know where?"

"If he's planning a major ritual, he's going to need the right kind of space," Neera said.

"A clear pathway to the heavens," Kami agreed. "Maybe they'll go to the top of the Gherkin. Maybe that's why he was there before, to scope out the area."

My mind worked through everything I'd learned, including a few nuggets of wisdom from someone writing her thesis on the function of space and rituals in ancient Britannia.

Much importance was placed on the right location. Proximity to the heavens was often a crucial factor.

Bingo. "I think I know."

"Tell me."

I whipped around, shocked to see Prince Callan in the Pavilion. He observed us with a murderous glint in his eyes.

"How did you get in here?" Minka demanded.

He snarled. "Do you know who I am?"

"You didn't hurt Treena, did you?" I asked.

He shifted his gaze to me. "What kind of monster do you think I am?"

I relaxed slightly. "Why are you here?"

"You said you needed me alive to help you." He spread

his arms wide. "Here I am. I'm going to kill the druid, but first I'll make him regret his choices."

I didn't doubt it. Even though his anger wasn't directed at me, I was terrified.

"The highest point," I said. "That's where the ritual will be."

Ione shot me a quizzical look. "Tower Hill?"

"No. The highest point in all of Britannia City. Westerham Heights." Thank you, Lucy.

"Everybody suit up," Kami ordered.

Minka winced. "Everybody? Someone should stay here in case..."

I placed both hands on her desk. "Let me explain the situation. If the druid manages to access the full power of the stone, he will become the most powerful practitioner of elemental magic *in the world*. He will be able to melt every building in this city with you in it. He will be able to command the Thames and flatten every hill that stands in his way."

"Let her stay," Briar said softly. "If it's as bad as you say, we'll need to leave someone behind who knows the full story." She looked at Callan. "It has to be a knight."

The vampire didn't argue.

Minka looked helplessly at the prince. "What about the royal army?"

"House Lewis needs to keep this quiet for political reasons," Callan said. "If our guards run riot over Westerham Heights, word will get back to our enemies."

"I'll get my bow from the armory," Neera said.

"Grab mine too," Ione called.

Stevie cracked her knuckles. "I think this druid will look just right with a sword through the belly."

Callan's gaze swept the room of enthusiastic knights.

"You're a violent lot, aren't you?" He tugged my elbow and pulled me closer. "Davina is safe, you know. That was the job. You don't have to do this."

I couldn't tell him about fears related to the stone—or to him.

I also couldn't lie.

"The queen asked for the stone."

"So she did."

I yanked away my elbow. "So I'm doing this."

His green eyes locked on mine and I felt a pulse of energy travel down my spine. "You don't have to wait until we've survived to ask me out, you know. Now is as good a time as any."

I recoiled. "You think I want to ask you out?"

"It's a natural response to imminent death. You fear you won't survive and you want something to keep you going in your darkest moment."

I snorted. "And you think a date with you would be enough to pull me from the jaws of death?"

He simply stared back at me with an amused grin.

My mouth opened and closed. I started toward the armory. A cache of weapons would keep me focused on the night's objective, one that did not involve a date with a vampire.

Callan followed me into the armory and whistled. "You have quite the inventory."

Swords. Daggers. Crossbows. Even a few pistols.

"How many knights are in your banner?"

"Seven."

"And you need all these?"

I shrugged. "Sometimes they get lost. Or broken." Or both.

"Excellent quality. Your friend—Lann, was it?" He

touched the blade of the nearest sword. "If it's a reservation you're worried about, I'm a prince. I have clout."

"We're back on this again? I am not asking you out."

"No?"

I shook my head adamantly.

"Hmm. Then what is it?"

How did I recover from this?

"Now it's my turn."

I blinked. "For what?"

"I have a question."

"No, I won't go to dinner with you."

"Why not?"

"Because."

"Fine, but it's not my question."

I cast him a sidelong glance. "It isn't?"

"What's your favorite dessert?"

My favorite dessert? We were about to take on a group of druids with a powerful magical artifact and he wanted to know about my sweet tooth?

"Chocolate." I paused. "With cherries."

He gave a nod of approval. "Decadent."

"You?"

"I don't care for dessert."

I reached for an extra dagger. "Liar. Everybody likes dessert, even if it's just cheese and apple."

"Are you calling the Highland Reckoning a liar?"

I drew myself up straight. "I suppose I am."

"Fine. You're right. It's creme brulee."

"French? How shocking."

"It's actually English in origin. Created in Cambridge but given a French name because it sounded better. You've never had it?"

I shook my head.

"One more question."

"You seem awfully chatty," I observed.

"I'd like to get to know you. I'd like to get to know the woman who saved my sister's life. Is that so unreasonable?"

He had me there. "I guess not," I mumbled.

"What's with you and animals?"

"I don't know what you mean."

He gave me an appraising look. "I think you do. The raven. The dragon. You shouldn't be embarrassed by it. It's an enviable skill. House Lewis could've used you during the latest werewolf uprising."

My pulse sped up. "There was a werewolf uprising?"

"It was a joke. The wolves are well in hand."

I wondered whether the wolf pack would agree.

"Is it magic?"

His question took me off-guard. "You think animals can only like me if magic is involved?"

He shrugged. "I've never seen anyone have the effect you do. I find it fascinating." He paused. "I find *you* fascinating."

I suppressed all possible responses.

He hooked an arm around my waist and pulled me close. The move was so unexpected that a gasp escaped me.

Even if I wanted to kiss him, I couldn't. It would be a betrayal of my species. There was also the vague worry that plagued me whenever I killed a vampire—that I might have just murdered a half-sibling without knowing it. It didn't stop me from doing what was necessary, but the thought was always in the back of my mind. As unlikely as it was that my mother had once knocked boots with Glendon, the Highland king, I couldn't wholly dismiss the possibility.

My response delighted him. "I take your breath away? Nice to know."

Callan's face was so smug right now. It took all my strength not to punch it.

"I'll take your breath away if you don't let go of me right now."

He laughed and released me. "I wish this weren't so serious. Otherwise I'd be having fun."

"I think you're managing to sneak a few chuckles in despite the looming terror."

A low growl emanated from him. "The looming terror is us."

A lump formed in my throat. I was glad to be fighting beside him and not opposite him, that was for damn sure.

He looked at me again and the hardness melted away. "We're about to ride into battle. Any last words?"

There was a momentary pause. "Grab a weapon, Your Highness. You're going to need it."

18

Given its location at the northwestern corner of the city, Westerham Heights wasn't easily accessible. I rode at the front of the top deck of a red double-decker bus that Callan had commandeered. It wasn't often that the entire banner traveled anywhere together. Fuel was expensive and we didn't have a suitable mode of transport. Enter one royal vampire with a fierce snarl and we were all set for the night.

The wind blew back my hair as I stared ahead at the black horizon.

"Can't this thing go any faster?" I yelled.

"It's a bus not a race car," Callan said. "Relax, we're nearly there. We'll get there in time."

Maybe so, but it wasn't a matter of being punctual. We actually had to stop him from completing the ritual.

I climbed down the spiral staircase. "Close enough," I called. I didn't want to tip off Dashiell that we knew the location. Let him be complacent.

Stevie parked the bus on the side of a dark stretch of road and we filed out with our weapons in hand.

"Sneak attack, my favorite," Kami said, smiling like a lunatic. Everybody had at least one crazy friend and Kami was mine.

"I thought this would be a steep climb," Neera said. "This hill is barely perceptible."

"It's the highest point in the city," I said. "It serves the druid's purpose."

"I'm disappointed," Ione said.

Kami groaned. "Fine. Next time we'll dump you off at the base of Mount Kilimanjaro. Have fun with that."

"Mount Kilimanjaro doesn't exist anymore," Ione pointed out. Some mountains failed to survive the Great Eruption.

I shushed the group as we approached a flickering light where no light should be. "He's there."

We crept low until we arrived at a clearing. Dashiell was crouched on the ground creating a stone circle. I gripped Callan's arm when I spotted the stone in the center of the circle. The vampire nodded in acknowledgment.

"Looks like he found a replacement for Davina," the prince said in a low voice.

I was so intent on locating the stone that I missed the pyre Dashiell had built in the background. I also missed the familiar woman tied to it.

I sucked in a breath at the sight of Mona.

The bastard had taken *my landlord*?

How? When?

There was no time like the present. Every minute that ticked by was one minute closer to the New Moon.

I charged ahead. "What did you do?" I yelled. "Go to my flat and kidnap the first person you found?"

Dashiell rose to his feet and smiled as though he'd been expecting guests and wanted to welcome them to his party.

"I went looking for you, yes. I thought it would be fitting if you took the place of the princess. An expression of gratitude for your interference."

"Such manners," Mona said from the pyre, plainly besotted.

"What did you do to her?"

"Nothing yet. Miss Mona was kind enough to let me in the building. You weren't there, of course. We started chatting and discovered common ground."

"And you decided she'd be peachy keen with being your victim?"

"She volunteered," Dashiell said. "You'd be surprised how many are willing to sacrifice themselves for the greater good."

"I don't see you with your hand up," I said.

Mona looked directly at me. "If it means the return of the sun and the end of vampire rule, then it's worth my life. It's worth a million lives."

Wow. I had no idea Mona felt so strongly.

"I can't let you do this," I told her. "There's more at stake than you realize."

Dashiell stepped forward and blocked my path. "I think you'll find there's more at stake than *you* realize."

He didn't fire a warning shot. The druid simply raised his hands and the earth trembled beneath our feet. Trees tore themselves from the ground by their roots and marched toward us.

"Imagine what I can do once the ritual is complete."

The other knights and Callan fanned out behind me and took on the trees while I tried to persuade the druid to stop the madness.

"This isn't the way," I insisted. As much as I understood

the desire to overthrow the vampires, this wasn't the right path. This druid craved power the way vampires craved blood.

I had to get that stone no matter what it took.

A bleating sound reached my ears and I froze. I turned to the side to see my pygmy goat tethered to a tree.

"Herman?" The flare of fear mixed with anger quickly morphed into a burning rage. "You kidnapped my goat?"

"Goats make excellent sacrifices," Dashiell said matter-of-factly.

I ignored him and pinned Mona with a death stare. "You went into my home without permission and *took my goat*?"

Sacrificing herself was one thing. Sacrificing my goat crossed a line.

"You can thank your big-eared cat for these marks." Mona held up an arm with bright red streaks. "He didn't appreciate my unannounced entrance."

Sandy had tried to defend the fort. Bless that temperamental fennec fox.

"A family could live for a week on that goat," Mona said. "You've been selfish to keep it as a pet."

"So it's okay to serve up a goat in the name of survival, but you hate vampires for surviving on human blood. Anybody else see the hypocrisy there?" I looked left to right. "No? Just me?"

Mona lifted her chin. "Do what you must, Dashiell."

"Mona, it won't do any good to hurt yourself. The ritual isn't effective unless they kill you. Suicide doesn't count."

"Why not? Isn't that even more of a sacrifice?"

"I hate to tell you this but I'm not even sure a human sacrifice will do anything. He's experimenting and he's using you to do it. Your death could be for naught."

"I don't care." Mona jerked her head to the side. "Why are you helping *them*? You're not a vampire."

I wanted so badly to explain my intentions to her, but I couldn't. She just had to trust me.

Kami stormed past me, moving too swiftly for Dashiell to stop her. She ripped the ropes from Mona and set her free.

Mona spat. "Stupid woman." She folded her arms. "I'm not leaving."

Kami threw the stout woman over her shoulder and started walking. Mona pounded on her back, demanding to be set free.

The ground shook again and a blast of air knocked Kami to the side. Mona fell to the ground and crawled out of reach. Dashiell hit her again with another gust of wind. She blew across the clearing and slammed into the trunk of a walking tree.

Dashiell turned and launched a ball of fire at the pyre setting it aflame. Everything happened so fast, I barely had time to register it, let alone react. As the flames licked the stalks of wood, Mona leaped onto the pyre. Her screams pierced my ears as well as my heart. I wanted to cry, to scream and wail, but no sound came to my throat. No tears filled my eyes. Mona had made her choice and it had been the wrong one.

A delayed scream tore from my throat. "No!"

"A noble sacrifice."

I whirled around to face Dashiell. "I think you mean stupid."

Dashiell extended a hand. "You're a smart and talented witch. Join me. There's still time to see sense."

"Sense boarded the station to LocoLand when you murdered your colleague and stole the stone."

Dashiell peered at me. "Surely you understand why that was necessary. You see what's at stake."

"I do understand," I said quietly. "Which is why I can't let you have the stone." I gathered my magic and compressed a piece of it into a small but lethal ball and let it go.

Dashiell disappeared and the magic smashed into the pyre instead, sending the flames even higher. The druid was wrapping himself in a blanket of air again and hiding from view the way he'd done on the rooftop.

I spun around and concentrated to see whether I could identify him by the intensity of the magic, but my detector was being thrown off by the stone.

"Where is he?" Callan demanded, swiveling left to right.

"Hiding, like a coward," Kami said.

I observed Briar as she untethered Herman and smacked his bottom to send him to safety. I hoped someone survived this to drive him home. Hell, I hoped I survived so he had a home to go to. If not, he'd end up in someone's stew.

I couldn't die.

Briar stilled. "What's that sound?"

Kami strained to listen. "I don't hear it."

"You will."

My veins turned to ice as I heard it. This time I knew what it reminded me of—the bending of metal. Instinctively I glanced at the horizon.

A creak and a groan reverberated. This time the sound was so loud that it shook the ground. Kami's eyes widened as she felt the shockwaves.

The ground trembled again and my heart skipped a beat.

"A horde of dragons?" Briar whispered.

"No."

Her brow furrowed. "Then why do you look like you need to change your underpants?"

"Because this is going to be worse." Much worse.

"Maybe you should reconsider that army," Kami told Callan.

A flash of metal appeared on the horizon. This metal wasn't melting.

It was walking.

Towering limbs—limbs made of towers rather than simply being tall—pounded the ground. At first I thought Dashiell had created metal monsters from Damascus steel, but it seemed he hadn't had time to master that particular skill. He was pulling metal from nearby buildings and reassembling them as monsters to do his bidding.

"If we knock them down, they're going to do damage," Kami said.

"If we let them walk, they're going to level the city."

Kami moaned in exasperation. "Why do we always have to make the tough decisions? Just once can't we be deciding between a chocolate or a powdered doughnut?"

I brandished my axe. "That will never happen. You know I'd go straight for the chocolate one."

"Fair enough."

Briar opened her mouth and roared. The ferocious sound made the hair on my arms stand on end. Even Callan paused to identify the source of the monstrous noise. Her magical armor melded with the night and a seven-foot-tall bear stood in its place. A nightmare covered in coarse, black fur. She dropped to all fours and ran toward the approaching monsters with surprising speed.

Stevie sliced through the darkness, a sliver of metal

glinting as she ran toward the circle. She was going for the stone. As a water witch, there was a chance she could control it, although I had every confidence the circle was warded.

Stevie reached the circle and blew backward as though flung across the clearing by an invisible giant. She landed on her back and skidded across the ground.

"I think it's warded," Kami yelled.

"You think?" Stevie rolled to her feet.

I turned away from the stone. A line of metal monsters pounded the ground as they approached the clearing. Two and three stories tall, they lumbered toward us and flattened everything in their path.

In that moment, Callan demonstrated how he'd earned his nickname. The Lord of Shadows peeled away from the darkness and revealed himself. I'd known he was with us, yet I'd momentarily forgotten. He lurched forward with his fangs on display. He was stealth and steel combined. Hard muscle and metal. I had to admit, he did my sword justice.

Part of me wanted nothing more than to watch him tear the monsters apart. I watched as he lifted the hunk of metal over his head, his muscles bulging, and used his head as a blunt instrument against an attacking tree. Holy hellfire. The way he fought. Precision. Power. The Highland Reckoning had it all.

In the circle, the stone glowed with a pale yellow light. Where was Dashiell?

"London!" Kami screamed. A sound I rarely heard and not one I welcomed.

One of the smaller metal monsters was standing on her torso and crushing her.

Fire. I had access to fire. The monsters weren't made

from Damascus steel. They were cobbled together from regular steel.

I whirled my hands in the air until they sparked with flames. I formed a ball the size of a cantaloupe and launched it at the monster's leg. It responded by lifting the leg and Kami rolled to the side. Briar Bear attacked the monster from behind. She wrapped her furry arms around the monster and squeezed until the monster fell apart. Pieces of metal dropped to the ground and scattered.

I hurried over to check on Kami.

She pulled herself to a seated position. "I'm okay. I'll heal."

Kami would say that if she were neck-deep in lava. Then again, so would I. We were cut from the same cloth of unhealthy independence.

"Can you control Dashiell?" I asked. "Reach for his mind. If you control him, you control the stone and all the monsters."

My mind control magic was limited to animals and it wasn't so much control as conversion. I won them over, whereas Kami locked on to a mind and controlled it until she decided to let it go. Then it reverted back to its owner.

Kami's face strained. "I sense it, but it's weak. I don't think he's close enough."

I shuddered as I pictured an army of metal monsters marching to take over the city. "We have to stop him."

Kami's blue eyes shone with sympathy. "Would it be such a bad thing if a druid used the stone to overthrow the vampires?"

I searched the murky clearing for Callan but couldn't pinpoint him. "We'd only be trading one master for another." The colonists didn't chuck tea into the Boston Harbor so they could be ruled over by the Cossacks. They wanted self-determination and they fought until they got it. One day we'd have to do the same.

But not this day.

Neera ran over, nearly out of breath. "Why is he the only one able to control the elemental magic from the stone? We're elemental witches and the stone is right there. Shouldn't we be able to harness some of it?"

Not when it was shielded by a ward of the druid's creation. Dashiell was smart. He didn't create the ward to just protect the stone physically. He created it for control. He wanted to prevent other magic users from accessing the stone's power. It was a failsafe in case we discovered his whereabouts, which we did.

The others couldn't break the ward of a druid.

But I could.

I had to be careful. If anyone figured out what happened, there would be questions.

Dashiell warded the circle before he'd fully accessed the stone's power. It shouldn't be impossible.

All I could do was try.

I spared a glance over my shoulder. Everyone was engaged in battle and there was no sign of Dashiell. Still hiding, you cowardly bastard.

I sprinted toward the circle.

"London, on your left!" Ione yelled.

An arrow whizzed toward me and I ducked. It sailed over my head and nailed its target. The bend of the knee of one of the metal monsters. The leg buckled and down the monster went. She must've spelled the arrow.

I kept running.

I reached the circle and stopped before I hit the ward like Stevie. The Elemental Stone sat in the eye of the circle, taunting me. No one was watching me. They were all too busy fighting. There was no time to waste. I used the corner of the axe to prick my finger and let a few drops of blood splatter on the rocks.

I forged a connection to the magic of the ward and *pushed*. The ward resisted. I pushed harder. I pictured turning a key, a sticky door, and then...

I stumbled forward as the ward broke apart and the circle admitted me. I scooped up the stone and held it against my chest. I felt a rush of power as the magical connection transferred to me. Incredible.

All at once the metal monsters and trees came to a halt. The cloak of air dissolved and revealed Dashiell. The druid stood at the edge of the clearing, observing the carnage from a safe distance. No doubt he anticipated returning to the circle for the stone the moment the last body was ground into the earth by the heel of a metal monster.

His face reddened and he staggered toward me in disbelief when he realized what happened.

"How? It isn't possible!"

Dashiell shook an angry finger as he advanced toward me. He didn't make it very far. I blinked and Callan was between us. He grabbed the druid by the neck, squeezing until I heard the telltale snap. He released the neck and let the limp body fall to the ground.

Slowly the other knights edged toward us with one eye trained on the frozen monsters. They seemed wary that our opponents might spring to life again at any moment.

"I have the stone," I announced. "They won't move now unless I will it."

Ione patted her right shoulder. "I think someone needs to reset this. It's out of socket."

Neera perked up. "Ooh! I volunteer."

Ione scowled. "You're my big sister. You shouldn't look so pleased. You know it's going to hurt."

Neera feigned ignorance. "That thought hadn't even occurred to me."

"You should keep hold of the stone," Callan told me. "Bring it to the palace tomorrow."

I peered at him. "You don't want to take it home with you now?"

"You were tasked with the assignment. I think it would make more of an impression if you delivered it to the queen in person. You can collect your fee then."

Why did the Demon of House Duncan care whether I made a good impression on the queen?

"I'll bring it tomorrow then."

"Very good. We'll expect you at ten."

I glanced in the direction of the bus. "Aren't you going to ride back with us?"

He hesitated. "I think I make the other knights uncomfortable. Now that the danger has passed, I think it would be best if I made my own way."

I didn't argue.

I watched in silence as he strode toward the black line of the horizon.

Briar shifted back into her human form and jogged over to me. Her magical armor was shredded and stained with blood but covered enough skin to preserve her modesty. "How did you do it?"

"His ward sucked. Too bad he couldn't create it after he had more power. Then it might've been a challenge."

Stevie joined our little circle, her expression quizzical. "I tried to break it."

"No, you tried to run through it. Not the same."

Kami limped over, clutching her stomach. "Briar, if you wouldn't mind putting those hands of yours on me..."

The knights gathered into a tight ball of relief and concern and focused on treating wounds. Their questions about me were quickly forgotten. By the time I snuck a glimpse at the horizon in search of the vampire, the night had swallowed him whole.

19

I arrived at the palace promptly at ten the next morning and silenced the alarm bells ringing inside me. This was it. One final interaction and then I'd return to obscurity where I belonged. My survival depended on it.

I was escorted to the throne room where I was left alone. No sign of Callan. Was I disappointed? Did it matter?

A moment later the doors opened and a disembodied voice announced the arrival of the king and queen. King Casek and Queen Imogen entered the throne room with the regal air you'd expect of them. Despite their role as heads of state, neither possessed the same level of intensity as the two princes. It seemed that Maeron had inherited his biological mother's and Callan had inherited his biological father's. No surprise the brothers clashed as often as they did.

"You must be our fair knight, Dame London Hayes," the king said, giving me a speculative look. He was an attractive man with kind gray eyes, a square jaw, and broad shoulders. He wasn't as tall as I expected. A smidge over six foot at most. I glimpsed a hint of silver in his hair. Only the oldest and most powerful vampires managed to acquire heads of silver. I should've been more frightened of him.

The queen placed a hand on his arm. "Knights don't use titles anymore, dearest."

I bowed. "Just London is fine."

"Thank you ever so much for the return of our daughter," the queen said. "I've told her she must learn to control her flights of fancy."

It seemed Queen Imogen still refused to admit that Davina had been in genuine peril. A parental weakness or an attempt to save face, I wasn't sure which.

The king eyed my satchel. "I understand you've brought us more than our daughter."

I opened my satchel and retrieved the stone. "As requested, Your Majesty."

The queen accepted it with a warm smile. "It will look lovely next to the other one. A matching set is always preferable." She glanced at her husband. "Isn't it, darling?"

She acted like they were bookends when she knew exactly how much power they packed. Did she think I didn't know or that I was too afraid to call her bluff? I mean, I *was* afraid, but it was still insulting.

"Your cooperation and loyalty to House Lewis has been noted." The king angled his head. "Pay the lady her fee, Nigel."

Yes, pay the lady before she glows silver in the middle of the palace and signs her death warrant.

A vampire stepped out of the shadows with a pouch and handed it to me with a slight bow.

"Thank you," I said. The bag was dense and I could feel the weight of the coins as I tucked the pouch into my satchel.

"Nigel will escort you out," the queen said.

"Not yet."

I turned to see Davina enter the room. In a yellow dress that brushed the floor and her golden hair in a French twist, she looked like a very different vampire from the one I'd met in the chapel.

"You didn't think you could come here without greeting me, did you?" Davina demanded, although she sounded more cheerful than angry.

Queen Imogen's gaze dropped to the floor. "Davina, darling, what have I told you about walking on the palace floors in bare feet?"

Ignoring her mother's reprimand, Davina hurried across the room and engulfed me in a hug. She was remarkably strong for someone who looked and acted like a princess. I stood there awkwardly with my arms squeezed against my sides and looked down to notice her pink painted toenails. I wasn't much of a hugger on any occasion, but I felt even more uncomfortable when the one hugging me was a vampire. The illogical part of me worried Davina would somehow sense my identity via osmosis.

"From now on, we're hiring you for all our knightly needs," she declared. "Isn't that right, Father? Mother?"

I stifled a laugh. I fully intended to add 'knightly needs' to my business card.

"I'd release her before she perceives you as a threat," another voice said, this one familiar and oh-so-intoxicating. "Trust me, you won't like the response. I've seen what she's capable of."

Callan swaggered into the room. Did he have to look so...so...? He flashed his fangs a reminder of who and what he was. There. That helped.

"Callan says you fought well," the king said. "You have no idea what high praise that is."

"The highest," Davina added.

The king regarded me. "How would you feel about a permanent post? I could use someone with your skills at Hadrian's Wall."

Hadrian's Wall? He wanted to send me north to be the first line of defense against raids from House Duncan?

The prince seemed to share my sentiment because he chuckled. "Her presence here is far more effective than at Hadrian's bloody Wall."

"Now that we've lost Victor, we could use someone skilled there," the king replied.

"Victor's death was unfortunate but unrelated to his post. Our knight's talents are best utilized here in Britannia City," the prince insisted. "Besides, my father is no threat to you while I live."

"I appreciate the offer, Your Majesty, but I have no interest in relocating. I have a life here." Small and manageable, just the way I liked it.

"If you change your mind..." King Casek began.

"She won't," Callan interjected. "She's very stubborn, as I've learned."

The queen smiled. "In that case, I'm surprised you both made it through the ordeal unscathed."

Same, girl. Same.

Davina clasped her hands together and flashed two dimples. "You should come for supper next week. London deserves a royal meal. Wouldn't you agree, Callan? She's skin and bone. I don't know how she manages to lift a weapon without injuring herself."

I suppressed a shudder. As kind and unexpected as the offer was, I needed to distance myself from vampires now.

"There's a fair bit of muscle in there too," Callan added. "She hides it well."

"Please don't feel obligated to feed me." There was no way I wanted to become a regular fixture at the palace. They were only nice to me now because I'd successfully completed a job for them. They were still vicious vampires at their cores. It wouldn't take much for them to decide to execute me on the spot, especially if they decided I was a threat.

And I most definitely was.

My magic flared in response to my thoughts, producing a few flecks of silver on the skin of my hands. I quickly clasped them behind me and ignored the rapid beating of my heart.

"Leave her be, Davina. She's a busy knight with more important considerations than which frock to wear to dinner." Maeron peeled himself off the wall. I hadn't even noticed when he entered the room. He must've made himself invisible until now.

Davina glowered at him. "You make me sound silly. You know I have loftier ambitions than food and fashion."

Maeron grinned back at her. "Of course. We wouldn't have bothered to save you otherwise."

I took a side step toward the door. "I'll leave you to your family time."

Davina waved a hand in my direction. "See? You've frightened her away. Why do you always do that, Maeron?"

"Enough," the king commanded. He shifted his gaze to me. "Go now before it escalates." He sighed. "Because it always does."

I bowed and hurried from the throne room. A soft silver glow emanated from my hands and I thrust them into my pockets. The faster I walked, the faster I returned to fresh air and freedom. The duty to House Lewis was fulfilled and I was free to return to the Circus. Thank the gods.

I almost reached the main doors without another interruption. Almost.

Callan appeared out of nowhere and intercepted me.

I swallowed a scream. "Why do you insist on walking around your own house invisible?"

He looked at me with something bordering on amusement. "Why so much interest in how I walk around my house?"

"It's bizarre. I don't walk around my flat invisible."

"Only because there's no one there to hide from, unless your animal companions are begging for food."

He wasn't wrong, but I didn't give him the satisfaction of admitting it.

Callan tilted his head in the direction of the throne room. "You've certainly made an impression on the right people."

"That's not why I did it." Not even remotely.

"Even so, it's good to have a royal stamp of approval, especially a knight like yourself in need of steady work."

"We're happy with the work we have, but I appreciate the thought."

His mouth curved in a smile that sent involuntary shivers down my spine. It was a smile that promised to make me feel things I didn't want to feel.

"Still not interested in working for vampires?" He glanced at the wall that featured a portrait of Queen Britannia with her fangs smeared with blood and her sword raised high. "I suppose I shouldn't be surprised. We can be a brutal lot." He turned back to me. "Then again so can you."

"I'm only brutal when it's necessary for self-defense."

"You don't think Britannia felt that way about her actions?"

I twisted to look at the portrait, clasping my hands

behind me and out of his view. "I have no idea what she felt." She was probably giddy with every vein she opened. There was a certain euphoria that came with bloodlust, one I hoped to never experience.

He leaned into me forcing me to bend backward or end up with my chest against his body. "Dine with us. At the very least I can promise it will be entertaining."

I frowned. "You really want me to come to dinner at the palace? With your family?"

"I'm simply repeating Davina's invitation. She's taken a shine to you."

"Davina would take a shine to a mirror if she liked the way she looked in it." I immediately regretted the statement. One because she couldn't see her reflection and two because she wasn't the airhead that Maeron accused her of being. She was tough and resilient and ridiculously sweet.

Callan seemed to sense my misgivings. "You don't mean that."

I brushed past him. "Like Prince Maeron said, I have a lot of work to catch up on now that I'm back to my regular duties."

He stepped aside and let me pass. "As you wish."

I walked out of the palace, half expecting him to follow. I pretended not to be disappointed when he didn't. The last thing I needed was a deadly vampire trailing me around the city. One look at me at the wrong time and he'd see me for what I really was.

I UNLOCKED the main door and climbed the five flights of stairs to my flat. The building seemed ridiculously small after spending time in the palace. I pictured the walls of my flat covered with paintings of myself like Britannia and laughed at the absurdity, although arguably my knee on Callan's neck in Hyde Park was worth capturing on a canvas.

Okay, I needed to imagine a scenario that didn't include His Royal Ruckus. He was a lethal vampire, plain and simple. Not someone to fantasize about unless that involved beheading him or driving a stake through his heart—assuming there was one beating inside his chest. Vampires like Callan were the reason the species was believed to be undead and devoid of functional organs. Cold. Menacing. Deadly. Those were the adjectives I had to remember when describing him. None of that devoted brother and hot, sexy beast crap. That way lies madness—and certain death.

I turned the key to my flat and stepped inside. No more Mona to stop by and check on me. The thought saddened me. On the other hand, maybe the next landlord wouldn't be a naive lunatic.

The flat was eerily quiet. The animals seemed to sense I'd had a rough time lately because they didn't come running. Instead they cast cautious glances from their respective locations on the floor, the sofa, and in the case of Hera, on top of the curio cabinet.

"I'm home."

The announcement was unnecessary. Every creature in my small kingdom had already gotten wind of my arrival. Even Barnaby was at the window. I crossed the room and opened it to let him in. Might as well let them all witness the final move in my playbook. Someone should witness my stroke of genius, even if it was only my speechless companions.

I dropped onto the sofa with a soft thud. My back was twinging and my legs ached. I peeled off my boots and examined my filthy feet. If the queen worried about Davina's bare feet on the clean floors of the palace, I'd hate to know what she thought of mine. I wiggled my toes. My body cried out for a warm, soapy bath. Five more minutes.

"I'm sure you're wondering why I gathered you all here," I joked. Multiple sets of eyes stared back at me, waiting.

I emptied the bag of coins from my satchel. I already had a regular hiding spot for valuables, but it was too small for my other acquisition.

I contemplated the Elemental Stone currently staring back at me from inside the curio cabinet. I opened the door and retrieved it. I needed a better hiding spot than in plain sight. It was too risky to leave such a powerful artifact on display, not that I entertained often—or ever.

My mother taught me the myths of many cultures when I was a child. One of my favorites was about Zeus and his mother, whose name she shared with mine—Rhea. My mother would be pleased to know I hadn't forgotten the story. Even more than that, she'd be pleased to know I'd copied one of Rhea's cleverest moments and made it my own.

In the myth, Rhea is fearful that her husband Kronos will swallow their infant Zeus because of prophecy. To prevent this, she swaps the baby and swaddles a stone to leave in his place. Kronos swallows the stone instead and doesn't discover the deceit until it's too late and Zeus grows up to overthrow him.

I crossed the threshold into the kitchen and opened the pantry. The flour container was the right shape and size. As much as I hated to waste the flour, it was the best option. I'd ward the container as well as the pantry door. Heaven forbid someone wanted to bake a cake in my kitchen.

As I submerged the stone into the remaining flour, the vibrations of magical energy tickled my skin. A vision flashed in my mind's eye. Symbols danced, suspended in midair like marionettes tugged by invisible strings. I didn't recognize any of them. I needed time to learn as much as I could about the stone. Maybe if I kept it close by for long enough, the stone would eventually whisper its secrets in a language I understood.

I secured the lid and hoped the decoy I'd left at the palace did its job. If my deceit was ever discovered, it didn't matter how much the Highland Reckoning wanted to get into my pants. I was a dead knight walking.

* * *

Don't miss **Three Dog Knight**, the next book in the series.

Books in the **Midnight Empire: The Tower** series include:

Wild Knight

Three Dog Knight

Deadly Knight

One Knight Stand

For more information about my books and to sign up for my newsletter, please visit my website at

www.annabelchase.com.

Other series by Annabel Chase include:

Pandora's Pride

Magic Bullet

Spellslingers Academy of Magic

Demonspawn Academy

Federal Bureau of Magic